Korean Folk & Fairy Tales

KOREAN
FOLK & FAIRY
TALES

Retold by
Suzanne Crowder Han

HOLLYM

First published in 1991
Seventh printing, 1997
by Hollym International Corp.
18 Donald Place, Elizabeth, New Jersey 07208 USA
Phone: (908) 353-1655   Fax: (908) 353-0255
http : //www.hollym.com

Published simultaneously in Korea
by Hollym Corporation; Publishers
13-13 Kwanchol-dong, Chongno-gu, Seoul 110-111, Korea
Phone: (02) 735-7554   Fax: (02) 730-5149
http : //www.hollym.co.kr

Hardcover edition ISBN : 0-930878-03-5
Paperback edition ISBN : 0-930878-04-3
Library of Congress Catalog Card Number: 90-85304

Printed in Korea

Preface

My first exposure to Korean folk tales was in the traditional way—word of mouth. It was about fourteen years ago when I was a U.S. Peace Corps Volunteer in a rural health center. At the time, a coworker-*cum*-friend, who spoke very little English and knew that I had to learn Korean, often told me Korean folk tales while we had coffee in a tearoom near the health center. I had long enjoyed folk tales so I found it a fun way to learn Korean as well as pass the time.

Over the years I have developed a keen interest in things Korean, especially Korean literature and art. I was thus very happy to have the opportunity to produce this collection of folk tales for Hollym.

I have tried to provide a representative sampling of Korean stories. Some of them are known in many versions and some can be traced to classical examples set down centuries ago. Some are peculiar to Korea and some are international in currency.

To facilitate understanding, some Korean terms, albeit romanized, are used and explained either in the text or in footnotes. Except for a few names, I have generally used the McCune-Reischauer system of romanizing. An introduction is included to provide some background about Korea and Korean culture and in the back of the book is a list of books that provided me much inspiration.

I would like to thank Mr. Chu Shin-won and Miss Uhm Kyoung-hee of Hollym for their patience and support and especially Mrs. Kim Miza, a very dear friend, for the advice and help she provided me in writing the stories.

Suzanne Crowder Han

Contents

Introduction

Dragons, ghosts, ogres, tigers, demonic foxes, supernatural spouses and, of course, people with all their human frailties are among the characters that populate Korean folk tales. Through them are revealed perceptions of life and notions about power, money, justice, love and interpersonal relations that through the ages have become ingrained in the Korean psyche. Passed on from generation to generation, the tales reflect the deep-rooted beliefs and customs of ancient Koreans and the creeds and codes by which they lived.

The major religions and belief systems which have shaped Korean society and the Korean ethos are Shamanism, Buddhism, Confucianism, Taoism and, more recently, Christianity. Shamanism is Korea's oldest belief. It attributes spirits, which affect the lives of the living, to all natural forces and inanimate objects like wind, rain, mountains, rocks and trees. Over all of the spirits rules *Hanŭnim*, Lord of Heaven, the Celestial Emperor of the Heavenly Kingdom. After death, good people are believed to become good spirits and reside in the Heavenly Kingdom and bad people are believed to become evil spirits and reside in the Kingdom of Darkness or the Underworld. Goblins are believed to be the spirits of good people who have died but for some reason have not been permitted to enter the world of the blessed and so wander through the world of the living. Ghosts, on the other hand, are believed to be the spirits of unhappy or wicked people who have been refused entrance into the other worlds and are awaiting their release from the world of the living. The Dragon Kingdom is an underwater utopia where only the very fortunate may visit for a very brief time.

The origin of Shamanism is lost in the haze of antiquity but it is without a doubt at the very root of the Korean psyche. It has influenced the spiritual life of the Korean people since time immemorial and all other religions and beliefs developed in a spiritual climate it dominated.

Buddhism, which was introduced to Korea around A.D. 372 and soon flourished because of its compatibility with Shamanism and other native beliefs, has the largest following. Its basic premise is that one's present life was determined by the past and what one does in the present determines the future. It was adopted as a national religion by the ancient Shilla (57B.C.-A.D.935) and Koryŏ (918-1392) kingdoms but eventually degenerated because of the luxury of temple life and the worldly ambitions of corrupt monks who meddled in politics, which accounts for the disrespect with which monks are often depicted in tales. It was suppressed when the Chosŏn Kingdom was established in 1392.

Confucianism became the official religion and philosophical basis for administration of the Yi Dynasty which ruled Chosŏn for over five hundred years, from 1392 to 1910. Society was divided into four strict classes—royalty, the aristocracy, commoners and the low born—and social mobility was virtually nonexistent. At the heart of Korean civilization were the government examinations called *kwagŏ*. Appointment to government posts, as well as the prestige and land that accompanied the position, depended on success in the examinations. Because the Confucian classics were the primary subject matter of the tests, strict adherence to orthodox Confucian teachings became a way of life. These emphasized loyalty and responsibility to family and ruler, ancestor veneration with its inherent son preference, self-discipline and restraint, the importance of learning, and the proper way to relate to others.

Unlike Confucianism and Buddhism, Taoism did not develop as a distinct belief nor did it ever flourish under official protection. Nevertheless, divination, geomancy, prophecy and other Taoist ideas and symbolism, especially those related to longevity and immortality, permeated Korean life at every level because Shamanism, Buddhism and Confucianism borrowed heavily from

China's religious Taoism. Even today people, even businessmen, often consult geomancers and fortunetellers about important matters and Taoist symbols are the most prevalent decorative motifs in the Korean home.

Korea has traditionally been a mat-sitting culture because of a unique method of heating by which a system of ducts beneath the floor carry heat from a kitchen fire or other source of heat. Houses traditionally consisted of a courtyard, or more for the wealthy, surrounded by high walls and one-story elevated buildings with open, wooden floored corridors on the outside where a person would sit to remove his shoes before entering through a latticed door covered with paper. Wealthy houses had a men's quarters, a women's quarters and a servant quarters.

Korea is a peninsular country covered with mountains and embroidered with rivers. The Korean Peninsula arches a little over 600 miles southward and slightly eastward from the southeastern corner of the Asian continent. Bordered by Manchuria and the Soviet Union to the north, China to the west across the Yellow Sea, and Japan to the east and south across the Sea of Japan and Straits of Tsushima, it was a strategic land bridge via which peoples and cultural developments from the Asian continent reached the islands of the Pacific in ancient times. It is thus only natural that an intermingling of currents from the surrounding countries are evident in Korean folk tales.

Animal Tales

Why Pig's Nose Is Short

One day a very long time ago *Hanŭnim** called for Chicken, Dog and Pig to appear before him. When the three heard this, they began to worry. On their way to the palace, each one thought about his past and what he may have done wrong.

"I command the three of you to go down to Earth and try to do something kind for humans," said *Hanŭnim* when the three came before him. "Do you understand?"

"Yes, Your Majesty, we will do as you command," replied the three in unison and they left on their mission.

On Earth each one exerted himself to try to do some work to help humans. Time passed and one day *Hanŭnim* called for the three to appear before him again.

"The three of you were sent to Earth to help humans. Please tell me what you did to help them."

Chicken spoke first. "I informed them of the time, Your Majesty."

"You informed them of the time?"

"Yes, Your Majesty. Every day at daybreak I crowed to let them know it was time to get up and start a new day.

**Hanŭnim:* the Celestial Emperor of the Heavenly Kingdom who rules over everyting including all heavenly bodies and natural phenomena, he rewards the good and punishes the wicked; he is never worshipped in the form of an idol.

If I didn't let them know it was time to get up, they would just sleep and never get any work done. Moreover, every day I provided them with eggs which they could use to make very tasty foods."

"Well, you certainly helped humans. And, because you did, I am going to award you this red ornament to wear on your head. Please wear it from now on."

"Thank you, Your Majesty," said Chicken in a humble voice.

"And what did you do for humans," said *Hanŭnim*, turning to Dog.

"I guarded their houses, Your Majesty."

"Why did you guard their houses?"

"In the day time humans go out to work and at night they sleep very soundly because they worked very hard during the day. I thus guarded their houses during the day and protected them from thieves during the night."

"Does that mean you never slept?"

"No, Your Majesty. I slept in the afternoon when humans were home doing their housework and having their meals."

"I see," said *Hanŭnim*, nodding his head. "You also worked very hard for humans. As a reward I am going to give you a fourth leg. Life should be much easier for you with four legs than with three."

"Oh, thank you, Your Majesty. I will be always thankful," said Dog, bowing humbly.

"All right, Pig," said *Hanŭnim*. "Tell me how you helped humans."

"*Kkul, kkul.*"

"What do you mean grunting like that? I asked you a question!" stormed *Hanŭnim*.

"I'm sorry, Your Majesty. I tried and tried to think of a way to help humans but everything I thought of, Chicken and Dog were already doing. No matter how hard I thought, nothing good came to mind. So, all I did was eat what humans gave me and slept."

"You no good swine! I ordered you to try to help humans but all you did was eat and sleep. You disobeyed me so I have no choice but to punish you." And with one swing of his mighty sword, *Hanŭnim* cut off Pig's long nose.

Ever since then, pigs have had short pug noses and go around sniffing and grunting whenever they are hungry, chickens have had red coxcombs and dogs have lifted their hind leg when urinating so as not to defile their gift from *Hanŭnim*.

The First To Be Served

Deer, Hare and Toad were invited to a celebration. When it came time to eat, there arose the question of who to serve first, it being customary to serve the oldest first.

"Well, I'm the oldest," said Deer, tossing his antlers proudly. "So I should be served first."

"Don't be ridiculous!" said Hare. "I'm the oldest. I must be served first."

"Just a minute," said Toad. "Instead of claiming to be the oldest, why don't you explain how old you are?"

"All right," said Deer. "I'm so old I helped nail the stars to the sky. So doesn't that make me the oldest?"

Hare laughed and said, "Well, I'm the one who planted the tree from which the ladder you used to nail the stars to the sky was made. So that must make me your grandfather."

Suddenly Toad began to sob. Deer and Hare looked at each other in surprise and asked Toad why he was crying.

"Well, it's just that listening to the two of you made me sad," explained Toad. "You see, I once had three sons. Each one planted a tree. The first used his tree to make the handle of the hammer you used to nail the stars to the sky. The second used his tree to make the plow that was used to dig the furrow for the Silvery River.* And the third used

---

*Silvery River: the Milky Way.

his tree to make an awl to bore the holes for the sun and moon. But all three died before the tasks were completed. So what you said made me think of my sons who died so long ago."

Deer and Hare said no more and Toad was honored with the first table of food.

The Bedbug, the Louse and the Flea

I n times beyond recall, Bedbug invited his two closest
friends, Louse and Flea, to his house to celebrate his
father's *hwan-gap*.*

Louse and Flea were more than happy to attend the
celebration for it was a great honor to be invited to a
hwan-gap party and there was nothing they enjoyed more
than a good feast. Happily they set out together to go to
Bedbug's house. They chatted for a while about the honor
he had bestowed on them and the foods they could expect
to eat and then lapsed into silence.

Soon Flea, who was very sprightly and impatient, was
far ahead of Louse who, being very portly and short-legged,
could not move very fast. Louse tried to go faster but he
could not keep up with Flea. The more he tried, the more
frustrated he became until he finally shouted, "Can't you
slow down? Honored guests should not rush."

Flea hopped back to Louse. "Yes, yes, you're right," he
apologized. "You see, it's just that I'm not used to moving
so slow." Flea's words annoyed Louse but still he was glad
to see that he was making an effort to slow his pace.

However, it wasn't long before Flea began to speed up
for he could envision all the delicious dishes he would be

___
* *Hwan-gap:* the sixtieth birthday, it is considered especially important as it represents the completion of a full cycle of the Oriental
zodiac, a great accomplishment before the advent of modern medicine.

served. Realizing he was outpacing his portly friend, he would slow down, only to speed up even faster when a hunger pain rumbled through his stomach. Finally, he lost his patience. "I don't think it is good for honored guests to keep their host waiting. So I'll go ahead and tell Bedbug you're coming," he said and hopped as fast as he could to Bedbug's house.

Bedbug welcomed Flea but was surprised to see that he had come alone. "I thought you would come with Louse," he said.

"Oh, don't worry. He's on his way. He just couldn't keep up with me," explained Flea. "I'm very thirsty. Please give me a bowl of wine," he said, eyeing the table laden with food and drink.

Bedbug gave Flea a bowl of wine and went out to meet Louse.

Flea, meanwhile, helped himself to the wine. And soon he was quite red in the face and feeling very jolly. He was singing and dancing when at last Bedbug returned with Louse.

"Here, my good friend, let me pour you a bowl of Bedbug's fine wine. You must be very thirsty after such a long walk," said Flea, handing a bowl to Louse. But when he poured, not a drop came out of the jug. Bedbug quickly handed him another jug, but it too was empty. Bedbug handed him another and another and another. But not a drop rolled into Louse's bowl.

"Why you swine! You drank all the wine!" shouted Louse and slapped Flea's face which was already red from too much drink.

Before Bedbug knew what was happening, his two honored guests were fighting. He tried to separate them by coming between them but he got banged and battered and finally fallen on.

The Bedbug, the Louse and the Flea • 21

And that is why to this day Bedbug is flat, Flea has a red face and Louse has a mark on his back where Flea kicked him.

The Secret of Toad's Appearance

O ne spring day a tiger awoke from a nap to see a large toad in a patch of grass below the boulder on which he was sunning.

"Oh, Toad, what are you doing?" he called out.

"Well, hello, Mr. Tiger. I'm enjoying this nice spring weather. Isn't it lovely! Just listen to those birds singing. It makes me want to do something special."

"Yes, I know what you mean," said the tiger, jumping down from the boulder. "Let's do something!"

"You got any ideas?" asked the toad.

"Let's see. What would be good?" said the tiger. After a while he sat up and said, "You know, in the spring man makes rice cakes and goes into the mountains to eat them and enjoy the scenery."

"Yes, that's right. They go on picnics," said the toad.

"Well, we can do that, too," said the tiger. "Let's make some rice cakes."

"All right," agreed the toad. "That's a splendid idea."

So the tiger and the toad set about making rice cakes stuffed with red beans, chestnuts, sesame seeds and jujubes. Happily they placed the cakes in a large steamer and put it on a fire to cook.

As a delicious smell began to come from the steamer, the tiger began to have second thoughts about sharing the rice cakes with the toad. "Let's have a bet," he said after a while.

"A bet?"

"Yes," replied the cunning tiger, "a bet would make things more fun. The winner gets to eat all the rice cakes."

This made the toad very uncomfortable. He could imagine what the tiger was up to. Yet, he knew that if he refused the bet, the tiger would become mad and eat him up. "All right. That's a good idea. What shall we bet?"

"We'll let this steamer roll down from the top of the mountain. The first one to catch it gets to eat all the rice cakes. What do you think?"

The toad knew that there was no way he could win but he had an idea. "Yes, it's a wonderful idea," he said flatteringly. "And the winner gets to eat all the rice cakes?"

"Of course. That's the whole idea," laughed the tiger.

When the rice cakes were done, the tiger and the toad took the steamer up the mountain. At the top, the tiger said, "Get ready! Go!" and gave the steamer a big push. Like an arrow, he shot down the mountain.

Rice cakes tumbled out of the steamer as it bounced down the mountain and the toad hopped down gobbling them up one by one. By the time he got to the bottom, his stomach was so full it looked like it would burst.

At the foot of the mountain, the tiger licked his lips as he picked up the steamer. He looked inside and frowned. With a roar he bashed the steamer on the ground.

"Well, were they tasty?" asked the toad when he finally reached the bottom of the mountain. "Did you eat them all?"

"It was empty!" roared the tiger.

"Empty?" asked the toad very naively.

"Yes! Completely empty! It made me so mad, I broke the steamer!" roared the tiger.

"That's too bad," said the toad. "If only we had shared the rice cakes from the beginning.... Anyway, I picked this up coming down the mountain," he said, placing a dipper of sticky rice on the ground in front of the tiger. "Let's share it."

The tiger picked up the dipper and scowled at the toad. "Do you expect the king of this mountain to eat scraps!" he roared and flung the dipper down on the ground with such force it bounced and hit the toad on the back.

And that is why the toad's back is covered with rice-like lumps and his stomach bulges.

The Ant, the Locust and the Kingfisher

Once upon a time, Ant, Locust and Kingfisher were neighbors. They often helped each other and sometimes shared a meal.

One day Ant was working very hard to prepare for winter. As he worked his thoughts turned to his good friends and the fun they had the last time they shared a meal. He was just thinking he would stop work early and invite his friends to dinner when he heard someone coming. To his great delight, it was Locust and Kingfisher.

"I was just thinking of inviting the two of you to dinner," he said with a laugh.

Locust and Kingfisher gladly accepted the offer and insisted they would bring a fish while Ant prepared the rest of the meal. After some discussion, they flew off toward the river.

Locust landed on a leaf floating on the water. Shortly a fish swam up to the surface and swallowed him, leaf and all. Immediately, Kingfisher, who had been circling above, swooped down, caught the fish, and flew back to Ant's house with it in his beak.

Once at Ant's house, Locust crawled out through the fish's mouth and the three friends began to feast. They talked and laughed and ate heartily.

"This fish is very good. I don't think I have ever eaten one so flavorful. How did you catch it?" asked Ant.

"Well, I just swooped down and grabbed it," said Kingfisher, puffing up his chest proudly.

"Now wait just a minute," said Locust. "You didn't catch this fish. I did."

"Why what do you mean? I'm the one who fished it out of the water and brought it here!" said Kingfisher.

"Well, you couldn't have done that if I hadn't waited on a leaf in the water to attract it to the surface!" shouted Locust.

"That's not true!" shrieked Kingfisher.

"It is!" shouted Locust.

"It isn't!" "It is!" "It isn't!" "It is!" The two argued back and forth.

Ant could not help laughing at them and his laughing made them argue all the harder. Locust grabbed Kingfisher by his beak and pulled so hard that it stretched. Kingfisher retaliated by biting his head. The sight of Kingfisher's unsightly beak and Locust's equally ugly head made Ant laugh so much that his waist became very thin.

And so that is why Kingfisher's beak is long, Locust's head is triangular and Ant's waist is thin.

The Rabbit's Judgment

L ong, long ago, when plants and animals talked, a tiger fell into a deep pit while roaming through the forest in search of food. He tried over and over to get out but the walls were too steep for him to climb and he could not jump high enough to reach the opening. He called for help but none came.

The next morning he called for help until he was hoarse. Hungry and exhausted he slumped down on the ground, thinking that he was doomed to die in the pit. But then he heard footsteps.

"Help! Help!" he cried desperately.

"Oh! A tiger!" said a man, peering over the side of the pit.

"Please! Please help me out of here!" pleaded the tiger. "If you help me, I won't forget you as long as I live."

The man felt sorry for the tiger but he was afraid of being eaten. "I would like to help you but, I'm sorry, the thought of what might happen makes me refuse. Please forgive me. I must be on my way," said the man and he began walking down the path.

"No! No! Please don't think like that! Please help me!" cried the tiger. "You don't have to worry! I promise! I won't hurt you! Please help me out! Please! I beg you! If you get me out, I'll be forever grateful to you! Please!"

The tiger sounded so pitiful that the man turned around and walked back to the pit. He looked around until he found a big log. "Here, climb up this," he said, lowering the log into the pit.

The tiger climbed up the log and came face to face with the man. His mouth watered and he began circling him.

"Hey! Wait a minute! Didn't you promise not to hurt me? Is this your idea of gratefulness? Is this how you repay a kindness?"

"What do I care about a promise when I'm starving! I haven't eaten for days!"

"Wait! Wait!" cried the man. "Let's ask that pine tree if it is right for you to eat me."

"All right," said the tiger. "But after we ask, I'm going to eat you. I'm awfully hungry."

The tiger and the man explained the situation to the pine tree.

"What do men know about gratefulness?" said the pine tree. "Why your kind take our leaves and limbs to make fires to heat your homes and cook your food. And it takes us years to grow big but when we finally do you cut us down and cut us up to make timber and planks for houses and furniture and the like. Moreover, it was a man that dug that pit. Gratefulness, indeed! Don't give it another thought, Tiger. You just go ahead and satisfy your hunger!"

"Now what do you think of that?" asked the tiger, smacking his lips loudly and slinking toward the man.

Just at that moment an ox wandered by. "Wait! Wait!" cried the man. "Let's ask that ox to judge?"

The tiger agreed so they explained everything to the ox and asked his opinion.

"Well, as far as I'm concerned, there's no question about what to do," said the ox, turning to the tiger. "You should eat him up! You see from the time we're born we oxen work diligently for men. We carry heavy loads on our backs and plow up the ground so they can grow food. But what do they do when we're old? They kill us and eat our flesh and use our hides to make all kinds of things. So don't talk to me about being grateful to him. Just eat him!"

"See! Everyone agrees. Now get ready to die," said the tiger, crouching to pounce.

The man thought that it must surely be his time to die. But then a rabbit came hopping by.

"Wait Tiger! Wait!" shouted the man.

"Now what?" roared the tiger.

"Please give me one last chance," begged the man. "Let's ask that rabbit to judge whether I should be eaten or not."

"Oh, what's the use? You know the answer will be the same."

"Please, please," pleaded the man.

"Oh, all right. But this is the last time. I'm starving!"

So the tiger and the man told the rabbit their story. The rabbit listened carefully. Then he closed his eyes and stroked one of his long ears. After a few seconds he opened his eyes and spoke slowly and deliberately. "I well understand what the two of you have said. But if I am to make a wise judgment we should go to that pit and you should tell me again what happened. So lead the way."

The tiger and the man led the rabbit the few short steps to the pit.

"Well it certainly is deep," said the rabbit, looking down into the pit. "Let's see, you say you were down there and you were standing here like this?" he said to the tiger and then to the man. "Well, get in the positions you were in at the time and then I can make a judgment."

Without giving it a second thought, the tiger jumped down into the pit. He was so hungry all he could think about was getting the decision-making over so he could eat the man. The man peered over the edge of the pit.

"So, that is how the two of you were. You, Tiger, had

fallen into the pit and couldn't get out. And you, Man, having heard his cries of help, came and helped him out. Now I can judge. The problem started when this man helped that tiger out of this pit," explained the rabbit as if talking to someone else. "In other words, if the man had not shown any kindness and had left the tiger in the pit, there wouldn't be a problem. So what I think is that the man should continue his journey and the tiger should remain in the pit. Now, a good day to the both of you," said the clever rabbit and he hopped away.

The Disobedient Frog

A young frog lived with his widowed mother in a large pond. A rascal and a trouble maker, he never listened to his mother and caused her much grief and embarrassment.

If his mother said go play on the hillside, he went to the seashore. If she said go to the upper neighborhood, he went to the lower. If she said do this, he did that. Whatever she said, he did the opposite.

"What am I going to do with that boy?" she mumbled to herself. "Why can't he be like the other boys? They always listen and do what they are told. And they're always kind and respectful. I don't know what will become of him if he keeps behaving like this. I have to do something to break him of his bad habits." Mother Frog sighed deeply.

"Ha! Ha! Ha!" laughed Little Frog. "Hush all that mumbling. You don't have to worry about me. I'm doing fine just the way I am."

"Is that so?" said Mother Frog. "Then why can't you croak properly? You don't even sound like a frog. Let me teach you." With a smile, she puffed herself up and let out a loud *Kaegul! Kaegul!* "Now you try."

Grinning broadly, Little Frog puffed himself up and let out a loud *Kulgae! Kulgae!*

"Why you impudent little rascal! You're going to be the death of me!" cried Mother Frog. "You'll listen to me if you know what's good for you. Now you..."

"*Kulgae! Kulgae!*" croaked Little Frog, hopping away.

Day after day Mother Frog scolded her young son but he continued to do as he wished and just the opposite of what she said. She fretted and worried so much about him that she became ill. Still he continued to misbehave.

One day she called him to her bedside. "My son," she said, "I don't think I will live much longer. When I die, please don't bury me on the mountain, bury me beside the stream." She said this because she knew he would do the opposite of what she said.

A few days later Mother Frog died. Little Frog cried and cried. "Oh my poor mother! I worried her so much by misbehaving. Why didn't I listen to her?" he scolded himself. "Now she's gone. I killed her. I killed her."

Little Frog thought about his mother and all the trouble he had caused her. Then he told himself, "I always did the opposite of what Mother said because it was fun. But this time I will do exactly what she told me to do."

So Little Frog buried his mother beside the stream, even though he did not think it was very wise.

A few weeks later there was a storm. It rained so much the stream overflowed its banks. Little Frog could not sleep for worrying that his mother's grave would be washed away. At last he went to the grave to keep watch.

In the pouring rain he sat, crying over and over, "*Kaegul! Kaegul!* Please don't wash my mother away!" And that is what he did every time it rained.

And ever since then, green frogs have cried *Kaegul! Kaegul!* when it rains.

The Ant That Laughed Too Much

In times gone by in a certain garden there lived a very wise and respected old ant. Because she had lived there for a very long time, it was not unusual for the other garden creatures to come to her for advice.

It happened that one day an earthworm sought her out. "Mrs. Ant, don't you think a young earthworm like me needs someone to take care of him? To prepare his clothes and meals? And, well.... You know what I mean...."

"You mean a wife," said Mrs. Ant, knowingly. "You need a wife."

"Yes. Yes. That's right," replied Mr. Earthworm. "And since you know so well what I need, would you do me a favor and find me a wife? A good strong one."

"Well, I don't know," said Mrs. Ant hesitantly.

"But you know everyone in the garden," pleaded Mr. Earthworm.

"Well, all right. I guess I could try."

"Oh, thank you. Thank you. I look forward to hearing from you. I know you'll choose wisely," said Mr. Earthworm and he went merrily on his way.

A few days later Mrs. Ant chanced to meet a young centipede. "Now she would make a good wife for that young earthworm," she said to herself, and made her way over to the multi-legged creature.

After chatting a while, Mrs. Ant popped the question.

"How would you like to get married? I know someone who would make a fine husband."

"Well, it is about time for me to get married," said Miss Centipede. "Tell me about this potential bridegroom."

"Well, he's earthy and hard working."

"Tell me more. What's he like?"

"He's long. Much longer than you. But he doesn't have any legs."

"No legs?" exclaimed Miss Centipede with a frown.

"Well, you see, he's an earthworm."

"What? You want me to marry a clammy, legless earthworm! Never! I wouldn't have the patience to make clothes for such a long body! Just think about what you're asking!"

"Well, now that you mention it, it is kind of funny," said Mrs. Ant and she began to laugh.

"The very idea. A centipede and an earthworm," muttered Miss Centipede, laughing loudly as she scurried down the path.

Mrs. Ant set off to find the young earthworm, laughing every time she thought about her proposal. She finally found him in the afternoon.

"Did you find me a wife? Did you?" he asked anxiously.

"Oh, yes," said Mrs. Ant, trying hard not to laugh. "A strong, healthy one."

"Good! Good! Who is she? Tell me! Please! Please!"

"Well, I found this lovely, young centipede," said Mrs. Ant, struggling to keep from laughing. "But she refuses to marry you. She says you're too long, that she wouldn't have the patience to make clothes for you. Ha! Ha! Ha! Isn't that funny?" Mrs. Ant burst into laughter.

"I don't think it's funny," said Mr. Earthworm indignantly. "Who does she think she is? I wouldn't marry her either. With all those legs, how would I ever be able to keep her in shoes! Why the very idea! How could you ever think of such a thing!" With those words he left in a huff.

Mrs. Ant thought this even funnier. She laughed and laughed. She laughed so hard she thought her sides would split. So she bound her middle tightly with a rope.

It was a long time before Mrs. Ant could think about the earthworm and the centipede without laughing. When she finally removed the rope, her middle was permanently pinched. And that is why ant's waist is very small.

The Tiger, the Persimmon and the Rabbit's Tail

A long, long time ago, a huge tiger lived deep in the mountains. His roar was so loud that all the other animals would hide when they heard him coming. He was so confident of himself that as he roamed through the forest he would roar out a challenge for any creature to match his strength.

Then one cold winter day, hunger forced him to leave the snow-covered forest in search of food. Stealthily he crept into the yard of a house at the edge of a village and looked around.

He saw a large fat ox in a stall near the gate. The sleeping animal made his mouth water. He crept closer to the stall. Then, just as he was ready to pounce, he heard a baby crying.

"Human babies certainly have an odd way of crying," said the tiger and, being very curious, he crept closer to the house. "He's really loud. How can his mother stand the noise?" he wondered.

"Stop crying! Do you want the tiger to get you?" shouted the mother.

"How did that woman know I was here?" the tiger asked himself and he crept closer to the house.

"Hush! If you don't stop crying, the tiger will get you," said the mother.

But the baby cried even louder, which angered the proud

tiger. "That baby isn't afraid of me? I'll show him!" said the tiger, creeping closer to the room.

"Oh! Here's a dried persimmon!" said the mother and the baby stopped crying at once.

"What in the world is a dried persimmon? That bratty baby stopped crying immediately. A dried persimmon must be really scary and strong. Even stronger than me," said the tiger and a chill ran up and down his spine. "I better forget the baby and go eat that ox before that dried persimmon gets me. I should have known better than to come to a house on a day like this. I surely don't want to run into that dried persimmon."

The tiger slinked into the stall and, since he was shaking all over, sat down to calm his nerves. At that moment, however, something touched his back and felt up and down his spine. "Oh, no!" he said to himself. "It's the dried persimmon. It's got me. I'm going to die for sure."

"What a nice, thick coat. And so soft," said the man who had sneaked into the stall to steal the ox. "I'll get a lot of money for this calf!" The thief put a rope around the tiger's neck and led him out of the stall.

"Oh my. What can I do? This is without a doubt that dried persimmon," moaned the tiger to himself. "Oh what can I do? I can't roar. I can't run. I can only follow it. Oh this is the end of me."

The thief was very happy to have in tow what he thought was a very fine calf that he could sell for a lot of money. Thinking he should get away from the area as fast as possible, he decided to ride the calf and thus jumped onto the tiger's back.

"That's strange," said the thief, "this doesn't feel like any calf I've been on before." He began to feel the tiger's body with his hands. "Oh my god. This isn't a calf. It's a huge tiger," he cried. "What can I do? What can I do?"

The thief was so frightened to discover he was riding a tiger, he nearly fell off. "Oh, I have to hold on," he said, grasping the tiger tighter. "If I fall off, that will be the end of me for sure. He'll gobble me up before I even hit the ground," he said, squeezing the tiger with his legs. "Just calm down," he told himself, "and try to think of how to get away."

"I'm going to die. I'm going to die," moaned the tiger as the thief tightened his hold on him. "What rotten luck to die at the hands of a dried persimmon! I must try to get him off my back. That's the only thing I can do," he said and he began to shake his body. Then he tried jumping and bucking. Over and over he shook and jumped and bucked as he ran but the thief held on tight.

After a while they came to a grove of trees. When the tiger ran under a large one, the thief grabbed hold of a branch, letting the tiger run out from under him, and quickly climbed through a hole in the tree trunk and hid inside.

The tiger knew immediately that the dried persimmon was off his back but he didn't even think about trying to eat it. He just kept running as fast as he could deeper into the mountain. Finally he stopped and let out a sigh of relief. "Oh, I can't believe I'm alive. I just knew that dried persimmon was going to kill me." He was so happy to be alive, he rolled over and over on the ground, smiling all the while.

"Oh Mr. Tiger," called a rabbit which had been awakened by the tiger rolling around on the ground, "why are you so happy? How can you be so happy in the middle of the night?"

"I almost died today," replied the tiger, "so I'm happy to be alive."

"What's that?" asked the rabbit, hopping closer to the tiger. "You almost died?"

"That's right," explained the tiger. "A horrible dried persimmon caught me. I've just this moment escaped from it."

"What in the world is a dried persimmon?" asked the rabbit.

"You fool! You don't know what a dried persimmon is?" laughed the tiger. "Why it is the scariest, strongest thing in the world. Just thinking about it gives me chills."

"Well what in the world does it look like?" asked the rabbit.

"I don't know," said the tiger, "I was so scared I really didn't get a good look at it."

"Well where is it now?" asked the rabbit.

"I think it must be up in a tree," said the tiger.

"Where is the tree?" asked the rabbit. "I think I'll go have a look at that dried persimmon."

"What? Are you crazy? As weak as you are, it will devour you right away," said the tiger.

"If it looks like it is going to grab me, I'll run away. After all, there's no one faster than me," laughed the rabbit.

The tiger told the rabbit the directions to the tree. "I'm warning you," he said as the rabbit hopped away, "that dried persimmon is a scary, horrible thing. Be careful."

At last the rabbit came to the tree. He looked all around the tree and up in the branches but he did not see any thing that looked scary. He looked again. Then he looked in the hole in the trunk and saw a man who was pale and shaking all over.

The rabbit laughed all the way back to where the tiger was waiting. He explained what he found, but the tiger wouldn't believe him.

"I'll go back to the tree and prevent him from leaving and you come see for yourself," said the rabbit and he left.

The rabbit went back to the tree and stuck his rump in the hole in the tree trunk to wait for the tiger to come.

"Come on, Tiger," called the rabbit when he saw the tiger

slowly approaching. "There's nothing to worry about. I have the hole plugged up."

When he heard this, the thief decided he must do something to keep the tiger from coming in the hole. He took some strong string from his pocket and tied it to the rabbit's tail. Then he pulled it hard to keep the rabbit from running away.

The rabbit shrieked because of the pain and the tiger took off running. "See I told you not to mess with that dried persimmon. Now the horrible thing has you," yelled the tiger.

The rabbit struggled with all his strength to get away. The harder he tried to run, the harder the thief pulled on the string. The rabbit finally got away but not with his tail—that was left dangling from the thief's string. And that is why to this day the rabbit has a stumpy tail.

The Dog and the Cat

In a small riverside village, there lived an old tavern keeper named Ku. He lived alone except for a dog and a cat which never left his side. The dog guarded the door and the cat kept the storeroom free of rats.

Ku was always kind and honest. He was also very poor because, unlike most tavern owners, he was very quiet and did not encourage his customers to drink until they became drunk. He sold only one kind of wine, but it was very good. People would come from the far end of the village to drink it and travelers often asked for a jug to take with them.

But there was something strange about Ku's wine. No matter how much he sold, he never seemed to run out. This was a source of curiosity for Ku's neighbors for they never saw any wine delivered to the tavern and they knew that Ku did not make any. They could not imagine where he obtained his wine. It was a secret that Ku shared only with his dog and cat.

Ku had not always been a tavern keeper. Many years before he had been a ferryman, ferrying people back and forth across the broad river which flowed beside his tavern.

One cold, rainy night, when he had just returned home from making his last run across the river, a stranger knocked at his door. "Please, Sir, could you spare a bowl of wine to help take the chill out of these old bones of mine," he asked humbly.

"Come in," said Ku. "My wine jug is almost empty. But you're welcome to drink what's in it." He emptied the contents of his jug into a bowl for the stranger. But the stranger poured a little of it into the jug and then drank thirstily.

"You have been most kind," said the stranger as he got to his feet. "I want you to have this as a token of my appreciation," he said, handing Ku a piece of amber. "Keep it in your wine jug and it will never be dry."

Ku turned the amber over and over in his hands for a while and then, with a laugh, dropped it into his wine jug, thinking he would have to fill it the next day. He ate a few pieces of dried fish and eyed the jug thirstily. "There must be a sip at least," Ku told himself picking up the jug. What a shock! The jug was full.

He poured a bowl and took a small sip. It was the sweetest, richest wine he had ever tasted. He drank a bowl and poured another. But the level of the wine in the jug remained the same.

Ku laughed heartily. "What a wonderful thing! The guy must have been a god! With this I can open a tavern! There will be no more ferrying back and forth across that damn river in all kinds of weather for this old man! I'll open a tavern! That's what I'll do! I will! I will!"

And that's exactly what Ku did and how he came to have an endless supply of wine.

But then one day something terrible happened. Ku picked up his jug to serve a traveler. It was empty. He shook it and shook it but there was not a sound. He was dumbfounded. The traveler left scratching his head as Ku wailed over and over, "It can't be! It can't be! I must have poured it out! I must have poured it into someone's wine bowl or jug! Woe is me! What shall I do?"

The dog and cat shared Ku's sadness. They sniffed all around the shop to try to find the amber.

"I'm sure I could find it if I could only pick up the scent," the cat told the dog.

"Let's look for it," said the dog. "Let's go through every house in the neighborhood. We must find it. He is so sad and unhappy," he said, looking at Ku.

So they began their search, determined to find the amber for their master. It was difficult and dangerous and took many days but they prowled through every house and shop in the village. They vowed to search the houses on the other side of the river when they could cross. Thus, when the river froze, they crept back and forth. All winter, they crept across to prowl the houses and shops.

At last one day when the river was beginning to thaw, the cat caught the scent of the amber and located it in a document box atop a chest-on-chest. But they didn't know what to do. If the cat pushed it off the chest, someone would hear them. Moreover, the box was too big for the dog to carry in his mouth.

"Let's ask the rats to help us," suggested the dog. "They can gnaw a hole in the box and get the amber out for us."

"Do you really expect them to help us?" laughed the cat.

"I know it sounds far-fetched. But we could promise not to bother them for ten years," said the dog.

"I guess it wouldn't hurt to ask them," said the cat reluctantly. "After all, it seems we have no other choice."

Surprisingly, the rats consented, but then they welcomed the chance to live without having to be afraid of dogs and cats. It took them several days to gnaw a hole large enough for a small rat to go inside the box and carry the amber out in its teeth.

The dog and cat thanked the rats over and over and then headed for the river. They took turns carrying the amber in their mouths.

"Oh no!" cried the cat when they got to the river's edge.

"The ice has melted! How can we get across? You know I can't swim."

"Yes, I know. That's a problem," said the dog. "I know," he said after a while, "I'll carry you on my back and you'll carry the amber in your mouth."

"All right. Let's go," said the cat, and it took the amber in its mouth and climbed onto the dog's back.

The dog walked into the water and began swimming. Presently he said, "Are you holding the amber tightly?"

Of course, with the amber in its mouth, the cat couldn't answer.

A little bit later, the dog again asked, "Do you still have the amber?"

The cat wanted to tell the dog not to worry, but with the amber in its mouth it couldn't.

"Are you holding the amber tightly?" "Have you dropped it?" "Do you have it in your mouth?" The dog asked over

and over, and, of course, the cat did not respond. As they came near the river bank the dog shouted, "Why don't you answer me? Do you still have the amber?"

The cat was so frustrated, it shouted, "Of course, I still have it!" And, of course, the amber fell into the water.

The dog was so angry he shook the cat off his back. Miraculously, the cat made it to shore. But the dog chased it until it finally escaped by climbing a tree.

The dog returned to the river and swam to the spot where the cat dropped the amber. But the water was too deep and murky for him to see the bottom. Then he walked up and down the bank where there were a number of men fishing. Suddenly he caught a whiff of the amber. The smell was coming from a fish one of the fishermen had just pulled in. Quickly he grabbed it with his teeth and raced away before the fisherman could catch him. Carefully he carried the fish home to Ku.

"That's a good dog," said Ku, when the dog dropped the fish at his feet. "We needed something to eat."

"What's this?" he cried when he cut the fish open. "I can't believe it! It's my amber! My amber!" he said jumping for joy. "You found it, Dog! You found it!"

Ku locked the amber in a chest and went out to buy a jug of wine so he could reopen his tavern. When he returned and opened the chest to get the amber he was surprised to find two money pouches instead of one, two jackets instead of one, and two combs instead of one. Everything he had in the chest had doubled. And thus Ku learned that the secret of the amber was that it doubled everything it touched.

With this knowledge he became richer than he ever dreamed possible. He made sure that the dog was well fed and often wondered what had happened to his other four-footed companion. As for the dog, he never again killed a rat, but he chased every cat that crossed his path.

The Hare's Liver

L ong ago the Dragon King* of the East Sea became ill.
The court physician read his pulse and then, looking
very grim, asked to call in several other renowned
physicians to consult with.

After reading the King's pulse, the physicians converged
in a corner of the room and could be heard mumbling, sigh-
ing and clicking their tongues. Presently, they approached
the Dragon King with bowed heads.

"Your Majesty, you are very sick," said the court physician.

"Confound it! I don't need you to tell me that!" groaned
the Dragon King.

"Yes, yes, of course, Your Majesty. It's just that... Well,
what we need to cure you isn't available in Your Majesty's
kingdom," explained the court physician, and the King's at-
tendants gasped. "To live, Your Majesty must eat the fresh,
raw liver of a hare, a land animal. That is the only thing
that will cure Your Majesty's disease."

"Send for one at once," said the Dragon King, turning
to his chief court minister.

"But Your Majesty, we sea creatures can't live on land,"
replied the minister and all the others nodded.

"Nonsense, there is one among you who can," said the

---

* Dragon King: ruler of the underwater world.

Dragon King.

"And that is I," said a tortoise, slowly making his way to the front of the ministers. "Being amphibious, I can survive on land. So I will gladly fetch a hare to cure Your Majesty's malady. However, there is one slight problem. Having never seen a hare, I do not know how to recognize one."

The Dragon King ordered the court artists to paint a picture of a hare. And, while the artists busily sketched and painted, the tortoise discussed his quest with the other ministers to learn all he could about hares. In no time at all, the artists presented him with a life-like portrait of the long-legged, long-eared creature. Tucking it safely inside his shell, the tortoise departed on his quest.

Swimming and floating, swimming and floating, he eventually came to land. He looked in all directions and headed for a picturesque spot, which from his perspective looked like a distant mountain. It was a lovely spring day. Birds and butterflies filled the sky and many animals crossed his path but not one looked like the picture.

Exhausted, he finally stopped to rest and to think of an easier way to find a hare. Unconsciously he stretched out his long neck and scanned his surroundings. As he did his eyes came to rest on a patch of clover and, much to his delight, the very object of his long search was in the middle of the patch nibbling the tender leaves and flowers.

"Excuse me," he called.

The hare quickly hopped away. But being very curious, he sneaked up behind the tortoise and, thumping on its shell, said in a loud voice, "Who are you and where do you come from?"

"Oh! It's you Mr. Hare. I've heard so much about you, I'm delighted to make your acquaintance. Utterly delighted. I'm Tortoise. I'm from the East Sea."

"Yes. Right so. I'm pleased to meet you, too. But may I ask what you are doing here, so far from home?" asked the hare, pleased that the tortoise had heard of him.

"Well, I'm sightseeing. You see, I had heard so many good things about your land that I wanted to see everything myself. It is nice but it doesn't compare with my home which is truly a world of beauty. By the way, have you ever visited the kingdom at the bottom of the sea?" said the tortoise.

"No, I haven't," said the hare.

"That's too bad. I would have thought a creature that moves as fast as you would have been everywhere," said the tortoise, trying to flatter the hare.

"Well, I have thought that I would like to go there at least once. I've been to a lot of places and it would round out my travels," boasted the hare.

"Then come along with me. I'll show you the most fantastic sights," cajoled the tortoise.

"But I thought it was impossible to go there," said the hare with surprise. "That's what everyone says."

"Yes, it is," said the tortoise, "but not if you go with me. I can take you there safely. It would be great fun. I could show you things more splendid than you could even dream about. Just think of the marvelous adventures you would be able to recount to your friends."

"Yes. Yes. That would be something to tell my friends," mused the hare.

"Just imagine how envious..."

"Enough! Enough! I'll go! I'll go!" exclaimed the hare.

"Just hop on my back," said the tortoise, trying hard to contain his excitement.

The tortoise lumbered back to the seashore with the hare boasting about his travels all the way. "Now hold on tight to my shell," said the tortoise and dove into the sea.

Finally they arrived at the kingdom on the bottom of the

sea. The hare was impressed with the dazzling sights and was thrilled to hear he would stay in the glittering palace and have an audience with the King himself. The tortoise left him in a room beautifully decorated with coral and shells, saying he would return after making the arrangements.

Presently a school of swordfish and a cuttlefish came into the room and said to come with them. The hare told them boastfully that he was going to have an audience with the King.

"Yes, we know. He's been waiting a long time," replied the cuttlefish.

"You mean he's been expecting me?" asked the hare.

"Of course. He's been anxiously awaiting your arrival," said the cuttlefish to the amusement of the swordfish.

"But why?" asked the hare in astonishment.

"Because of your good liver," said the cuttlefish, wrapping a long tentacle around the hare. "Your good liver," he chuckled.

"But I don't understand," said the hare, beginning to feel uncomfortable.

"You will soon," said the cuttlefish. "Now be quiet!"

Presently they came to a large pearly door. "Well, here we are. Now follow me and show some respect," said the cuttlefish as the door swung open. "Your Majesty, King of the Sea and all that reside therein," his voice boomed out, "here is the hare."

The hare looked up and almost fell over in shock at finding himself before the Dragon King. He was so scared his pink ears quivered.

"Welcome to my kingdom," said the Dragon King in a hoarse voice. "As I am dying, I must forego formality and get down to the business at hand. Tortoise brought you here so that I can eat your liver. It is the only cure for my illness. However, do not feel sad. After all, it is not as if your death would be in vain. It is for a good cause; my salvation. You will be honored with an elaborate funeral and a magnificent monument will be erected as a memorial to you. Just consider yourself fortunate to have died for a just cause rather than as the prey of a hunter or some beast of the forest. Now get ready to die a noble death."

The hare knew that he had to remain calm. He bowed deeply to the Dragon King and then, to have time to think of a way to save himself, he bowed to all the nobles surrounding the Dragon King and to the swordfish guards standing ready to slay him. "Your Majesty," he finally said, bowing to the Dragon King again. "I would gladly sacrifice myself to perpetuate your life. Unfortunately, to slit open my belly now would not do either of us any good because my liver is not with me."

"What?" roared the Dragon King. "Do you expect me to believe that?"

"But it's true, Your Majesty. Because my liver has special curative powers, it is always in great demand as a panacea. So I often hide it. I use it mostly at night and keep it hidden in the daytime. If Tortoise had only told me of Your Majesty's need, I would have gladly brought it."

"Do you think I am a fool? It's impossible to take one's liver in and out at will. Isn't that right?" said the Dragon King, turning to his court ministers.

"Yes, Your Majesty. Completely impossible," they chorused.

"Look, Your Majesty, look at my mouth. No other creature has a mouth like mine. That's because no other creature can take its liver in and out. And that's why my upper lip is split," said the hare. The great hall was silent. "Now, if it would please Your Majesty, I would gladly go get my liver if Tortoise will take me home. But we must go quickly or else Your Majesty might... I don't dare say the word," said the hare, lowering his head in a show of sorrow.

"Tortoise," the Dragon King finally spoke, "Take the hare to get his liver. And please hurry."

The tortoise and the hare departed at once. The hare danced for joy when the tortoise finally crawled out of the water onto a sandy beach. He laughed and laughed until he thought his liver really would come out his mouth.

"I know you must be happy to be home again," said the tortoise after catching his breath. "But please get your liver. We really must hurry back to the Dragon King."

"You stupid tortoise! Despite your thousand years, you believe I can take my liver in and out. Ha! Ha! Ha! You thought you would trick me but I fooled you," said the hare and hopped away, laughing boisterously.

The tortoise wept as he thought about his dying King. He knew there wasn't enough time for him to capture another hare and deliver it to him.

Suddenly a god with a long white beard and flowing garments appeared and said in a resonant voice, "Don't despair. I will help you for I admire your faithfulness and perseverance. Take these ginseng roots to your King. They will cure his illness and restore his health."

The tortoise thanked him and hurried back to the Dragon King's palace. The Dragon King ate the roots and became well. He made the tortoise his special attendant and the highest-ranking minister in his court.

The Rabbit and the Old Tiger

One day a long time ago, an old tiger roamed the dell in search of food. To his delight, he espied a rabbit munching on clover and so he quietly walked up to him.

"Well, Mr. Rabbit, am I glad to see you. You're just what I had in mind for breakfast," said the tiger and he opened his mouth wide.

"Wait! Wait!" cried the rabbit. "I don't think you would find me very tasty. See how skinny I am. I'll make you some special rice cakes. Let me get them." And with that the rabbit hopped behind a large rock and gathered up some small white stones.

"Here we are," said the rabbit, hopping back to the tiger.

"How do you eat them?" asked the tiger.

"Well, usually you just eat them as they are. But these are a little hard since I've had them several days so I'll build a fire to toast them. They're even more delicious toasted," explained the rabbit, and he began gathering twigs.

Once the fire was started, he put the stones on it and said, "Now don't those look good. There's five for you and five for me." A few moments later he said, "Oh, I almost forgot the soy sauce. That will really bring out the flavor in them. I'll be back in a jiff. Don't eat any until I return," he said and hopped away.

The tiger stared at the stones glowing in the fire. He licked his lips and counted them. He smiled and counted them again. Then he laughed and said to himself, "That stupid rabbit. He can't even count. He said there are ten rice cakes but there are eleven. I'll just have one now and he'll never know one is missing."

He took the reddest one, popped it into his mouth and gulped it down. His eyes became large as it burned all the way down to his stomach. He ran to the nearest stream and drank and then retreated to his cave. It was a long time before he was able to eat.

One day, after he recovered, he was looking for food when he chanced to meet the rabbit again. "Now I've got you," the tiger shouted. "I've been waiting to sink my teeth into you for a long time!"

"Wait! Wait!" cried the rabbit, trying to think of a way to escape. "Wouldn't you rather have some tasty sparrows?" he said, looking up at some flying above them. "They're really tasty this time of year."

Tiger looked up at the sparrow-filled sky. "Well, it has been a long time since I had bird," he said, licking his lips.

"Then that settles it," said the rabbit. "You just do what I say and you'll have a true feast. You..."

"This isn't another one of your tricks, is it? For if it is, you're..."

"No, no, no. Don't worry. Just do what I say," said the rabbit. "See those bushes over there. Just go sit in the middle of them and look up at the sky with your mouth open wide. I'll drive the sparrows into your mouth."

The tiger loped to the bushes, happily thinking about the feast of birds he would soon enjoy. He sat down, looked up at the sky and opened his mouth as wide as he could.

"That's good. Don't move," called the rabbit as he set fire to the bushes. "Don't move. They're coming your way. Keep your mouth open," he shouted and scampered off.

"Oh, great! I can hear them twittering," said the tiger to himself as the fire crackled around him. "But what's that smell and why am I so hot?"

"I give up, I'm too hot," the tiger shouted and finally looked down. He saw the raging fire and took off running. He survived the rabbit's trap but his coat was so badly scorched that he had to remain in his cave until it grew back.

Then one cold winter day when he went to a stream for a drink he met the rabbit again.

"Oh, good! Supper!" said the tiger, opening his mouth wide.

"Wait!" shouted the rabbit.

"No! You've played your last trick! I'm going to eat you this time!" roared the tiger.

"Please, Mr. Tiger. I was only trying to help you. You just didn't do what I said," pleaded the rabbit. "Now I'm willing to help you again. But, then, I guess you wouldn't be interested in what is probably the most delicious food this time of year. So, I'll..."

"What's that?" said the tiger, his curiosity perked.

"Fish, of course," said the rabbit. "There's nothing better this time of year than a nice fat fish. And this stream is full of them."

"How do you catch them?" asked the tiger.

"Well, I have to sit here and wait for them to jump out of the stream. But you, Mr. Tiger, you wouldn't have to do that."

"Why's that?" asked the tiger.

"Your tail," replied the rabbit. "It's very long so all you need to do is sit on the bank with your tail in the water and wait for a fish to take hold of it. Come to think of it, it is so long, you could wait for several fish to grab it before you pull it out."

"Well, I guess I could give it a try," said the tiger, "But

if this is another trick..."

"No, no. You needn't worry," said the rabbit. "I'll even help you with the fishing. I'll go up stream and make some noise to scare the fish so they'll swim down this way."

"All right," said the tiger. "Let's do it. I'm hungry."

"Okay. Sit down on the bank with your tail in the water and wait. But remember, you mustn't move or make a sound," explained the rabbit and scampered away.

The tiger sat very still and quiet. Presently the sun set and the water began to freeze. The tiger's tail began to feel heavy and the thought of succulent fish made his mouth water. Although he felt very cold, he sat very still, saying over and over to himself, "This is wonderful. Soon I'll have enough fish that I can feast for days."

Finally, when the moon came out, the greedy tiger said, "I think I've caught enough. And I'm really hungry." He tried to pull his tail out but it wouldn't come. "I've caught so many fish I can't get my tail out," he said to himself as he turned to look at his fish-laden tail but to his horror he saw that the stream had frozen and his tail was stuck fast. He pulled harder and harder but his tail wouldn't come out.

At sunrise, a hunter came along and discovered the tiger and soon his skin was hanging on a wealthy man's wall.

The Vanity of the Rat

T here once was a rat couple who had only one child, a daughter. And, as one would guess, they doted on her. Of course, when it came time for her to marry, they wanted only the best husband for her.

They thought about all the rats they knew but decided none of them were good enough for their daughter.

Then one day Mr. Rat said to Mrs. Rat, "I know who will make a perfect husband for our little darling. The sun."

"The sun?" asked Mrs. Rat. "Why do you think the sun will be a good husband for her?"

"Because there is none more powerful in the world than the sun."

"Yes, yes. The sun is the most powerful. He's magnificent. Let's ask him at once," said Mrs. Rat, ecstatically.

The two went out into their garden where the sun was beaming down. "Oh, Mr. Sun! Mr. Sun!" they called, trying to keep their eyes open as they looked up into the sky.

"Yes, yes. What can I do for you?" replied the sun.

"My wife and I would like to offer you our daughter's hand in marriage," said Mr. Rat proudly.

"I'm honored," said the sun, "but why do you want me to marry her?"

"Because you are so powerful and magnificent," said Mr. Rat and Mrs. Rat nodded in agreement.

"Well, I'm pleased that you think so highly of me," said

Mr. Sun, "but I must confess that there is one more powerful than me."

"And who might that be?" said Mr. Rat with surprise.

"Why Mr. Cloud, of course. I am powerless when he covers me."

"Yes. Right so. Right so," said Mr. Rat, nodding over and over. "Come, my dear," he said, taking Mrs. Rat by the hand, "let's go see Mr. Cloud."

They climbed a nearby mountain over which a big, billowy cloud hung in the sky. They called to Mr. Cloud and, telling him what they had heard from Mr. Sun, offered him their daughter's hand in marriage.

But Mr. Cloud said, "What Mr. Sun told you is right. However, I am powerless when I meet Mr. Wind. Wherever he blows, I must go."

"Yes, yes. Of course. Of course," said Mr. and Mrs. Rat and they went off to find Mr. Wind.

Coming down the mountain, they found Mr. Wind in a grove of pines. "I am strong," he told them on hearing their story. "I can make a big tree topple over or blow down a house. I can even churn up the ocean. But try as I may, I cannot budge a stone Buddha. I am powerless before a stone Buddha."

"Then we'll just have to ask a stone Buddha," said Mr. Rat and he and Mrs. Rat hurried on down the trail to see a stone Buddha standing near their village.

"Well I'm flattered that you want me to marry your daughter," said Mr. Stone Buddha, "but I don't think I'm right for her either. Of course I'm strong and Mr. Wind can't move me. But I am by no means the strongest in the world. There is someone that can make me fall over quite easily. Oh, the thought just frightens me."

"Please, Mr. Stone Buddha. Please tell us who," said Mr. Rat.

"Well," said Mr. Stone Buddha, "it is none other than you and your cousins the moles. Your race is really strong. Why if one of you burrows under my feet I'll topple right over. Yes indeed, you rats are a really strong breed. I'm no match for you."

"Thank you. You've been very helpful," said Mr. Rat, trying to hide his embarrassment.

And so that is why the rat's daughter married a rat.

Two Frogs

O nce upon a time there were two frogs who were bored with their surroundings. One lived in a bog in Chŏlla-do Province and the other lived in a pond in Kyŏngsang-do Province.

The two frogs lived far apart, and neither knew that the other existed. Yet, one day, they both had the same thought.

"I think I will go see what is on the other side of that mountain," said Chŏlla-do Frog. "Surely life is more interesting in Kyŏngsang-do than here."

"Life is so boring here," said Kyŏngsang-do Frog. "It must be better on the other side of that mountain. I think I will go see what Chŏlla-do is like."

So, on the same day, both frogs set out to explore what was on the other side of the mountain. The way was harder and longer than either frog had expected. But each hopped on and on, each thinking that the other side of the mountain must be a more interesting and better place to live. At last, after many days, they reached the top of the pass and each was shocked to see the other.

"Where are you from and where are you going?" asked Kyŏngsang-do Frog.

"Well, I'm from Chŏlla-do and I'm crossing this mountain to see what Kyŏngsang-do is like," replied Chŏlla-do Frog.

"What a coincidence!" said Kyŏngsang-do Frog. "I'm from

Kyŏngsang-do and I'm on my way to see Chŏlla-do."

The two frogs laughed and then sat down to rest. "It's certainly a tiring trip," said Chŏlla-do Frog with a sigh. "If I could just get a glimpse of where I'm going, the rest of the trip might seem easier."

"Yes, I feel the same way," said Kyŏngsang-do Frog. "If only we were taller, we might be able to see both from here."

"Let's stand on our hind legs and balance each other with our front legs so that we can lift our heads way up and perhaps we will be able to get a glimpse of where we are going," said Chŏlla-do Frog.

"That's a good idea," said Kyŏngsang-do Frog. "Let's give it a try."

So the two stood on their hind legs, Chŏlla-do Frog facing Kyŏngsang-do and Kyŏngsang-do Frog facing Chŏlla-do, and looked over each other's shoulder. But the foolish frogs did not realize that in this position their big, bulgy eyes would see behind them instead of in front.

"How strange!" said Chŏlla-do Frog. "Kyŏngsang-do isn't anything special. It looks just like Chŏlla-do."

"Yes, it's amazing!" said Kyŏngsang-do Frog. "I thought Chŏlla-do would be different. But it's no different from Kyŏngsang-do. I may as well go back home."

"Yes, me too," said Chŏlla-do Frog. "It's hardly worth the bother. It seems that everywhere is just the same so I guess home is the best place for me."

So the two frogs returned home and lived happily ever after, each believing that the two provinces were as alike as two lily pads.

Ghosts, Goblins and Demons

The Singing Lump

I n a small mountain village there lived a kind old man who had a huge tumor on the right side of his face. Although it caused him much discomfort, he was always cheery and hummed or sang a song wherever he went. He was well liked by the villagers and they fondly referred to him as Old Man Lump.

One day Old Man Lump went to gather wood on a mountain which was a little far from the village. He climbed up to a thick grove of trees where he could gather a lot of branches and then sat down for lunch. After his meal he set to work, happy to see so many fallen limbs. He worked very hard and before he knew it, darkness was enclosing the ridge.

He started down the mountain but he slipped and fell several times because he could not see the path. "I guess I should just find a place to sleep in this forest and return home in the morning," he told himself.

He walked through the forest, looking every direction in the hope of spotting some place where he could take shelter for the night. Finally, he saw a light in the distance.

He walked toward the light and came to a small hut in a glade.

"Anyone home?" he called. There was no answer. "Well, I'll just go in and wait for the owner to return."

He entered the hut and sat down to await the owner's return. He waited for what seemed like a long time and finally, being very tired, he lay down to sleep. But sleep would not come and he twisted and turned on the cold floor. Presently he sat up and began to sing.

He was singing a very lovely song when suddenly he heard the sound of shuffling feet outside. He jumped up and opened the door, thinking the owner had returned.

"Was that you singing, Old Man?" gruffly asked a fat, horned creature which the old man knew must be a *tokkaebi** of which he had heard tales since childhood.

"Yes," Old Man Lump timidly replied.

"Where does it come from?" "How do you do it?" "Can you teach us?" called the pack of *tokkaebis.*

"Be quiet! I'll ask the questions!" shouted what appeared to be the leader. "Now, Old Man, tell me from where your lovely song comes?"

"Well, from my throat, of course," said Old Man Lump.

"Your throat?" cried the *tokkaebis*, and they muttered among themselves.

"Now just a minute," said the leader. "We all have throats too but beautiful songs do not come out. You better tell us where your beautiful song comes from or you will wish you had never met us."

Old Man Lump was scared. He did not know what to say. He rubbed his chin and touched his lump as he tried to think. Suddenly a smile spread across his face. "All right. If you must know," he said, trying to sound reluctant, "it comes from this lump on my cheek."

"Well, then," said the head *tokkaebi*, "you must give that wonderful thing to us."

"Oh, I would if I could," Old Man Lump said sadly. "But as you can see, it is stuck to my cheek."

---

* *Tokkaebi:* mischievous horned goblin which is human-like and not particularly malevolent but temperamental and easily angered.

"That's no problem," laughed the *tokkaebi*. "You take this," he said, thrusting a heavy bag into Old Man Lump's hands, "and I'll take this," he said, grabbing the lump.

Before Old Man Lump knew what was happening, the *tokkaebis* were racing into the forest, laughing loudly.

Old Man Lump rubbed his cheek. He couldn't believe it. The lump was gone. He jumped for joy and then he remembered the bag. He opened it and was delighted to find it filled with sparkling jewels and gold and silver coins and nuggets.

With the first rays of sunlight he set out for home. Everyone stared at him as he walked through the village and children skipped about shouting gleefully, "Old Man Lump has lost his lump!"

News of Old Man Lump's good fortune spread throughout the village as he shared his wealth with his neighbors. It wasn't long before the story was being repeated in other villages in the valley.

"That's unbelievable," said a mean, avaricious man living in a neighboring village. "I would do anything to get rid of this lump," he said, rubbing a big ugly tumor on the left side of his face. "I'll just have to pay a visit to that old man." But his neighbors knew that what he was really interested in was getting a bag of gems and gold.

Seeing the lump on the man's face, Old Man Lump felt sorry for him, remembering how he himself had suffered. He told the man the whole story.

"Where did you say that hut was?" asked the man. Old Man Lump explained and the man rushed off without even a word of thanks.

The man found the hut and, on entering, immediately began to sing in a very loud voice. Visions of gold and silver filled his head as his song echoed through the forest.

Presently he heard footsteps in the yard and began to

sing even louder.

"So, you've returned," shouted a *tokkaebi*, pulling open the door.

Before the man could speak, the room was full of *tokkaebis* and they were circling him.

"Welcome. Welcome," said the man. "I was hoping you would stop by. You see I want to sell you my singing lump."

"Did you hear that?" laughed the head *tokkaebi*. "He wants to sell us his singing lump. What do you think, guys, shall I pay the man?"

"Yes! Yes! Pay him! Pay him!" they all laughed.

"Here you are," said the head *tokkaebi*, reaching for the man's cheek. "Here's a lump to go with your other one!" he shouted and stuck Old Man Lump's tumor on the man's cheek and raced into the forest with all the other *tokkaebis* laughing boisterously.

The man fell down on the ground and cried loudly. Because of his greediness, he now had two ugly lumps pulling at his cheeks instead of one.

The *Tokkaebi's* Club

L ong, long ago there were two brothers who lived in a small mountain village. The oldest was wealthy and very selfish and irresponsible while the youngest was poor and very kind and diligent.

Younger Brother took care of his elderly parents because Older Brother refused, even though it was his duty as the oldest son. Every day Younger Brother went into the forest to gather wood to sell in order to buy food for them.

One day he went deeper into the forest than usual. He worked hard most of the morning and afternoon for the ground was covered with fallen branches. He gathered the branches into piles, thinking that he would collect them in the next few days. Finally he sat down to rest with his back against a tree and was soon dozing.

Plop! Something hit the top of his head.

"What was that?" he said, rubbing his head. Then he noticed a hazelnut on the ground beside him. "Oh, this will be a tasty treat for Father," he said, picking it up and putting it into his pocket.

He leaned back against the tree and thought about how happy his father would be to get the tasty nut. Then another nut fell on the ground beside him. "That's good," he told himself, picking it up, "I'll give this one to Mother." A few minutes later, two nuts fell at the same time. "I'll take these to my brother and his wife," he said, picking them up.

Another fell and he picked it up, saying "This one is for me."

He looked up at the top of the tree and saw that the sky was filled with dark clouds. Quickly he gathered up his things and headed down the trail. But he had not gone very far when big rain drops began pelting him. "I better take shelter somewhere, I'll never make it down the mountain in this rain."

After what seemed like hours, he spotted a rundown house a short distance from the path. At the edge of the clearing he called, "Anyone home?" But there was no answer. When he got closer, he realized that it was an abandoned house and very dilapidated. He went inside and lay down on the floor. He fell asleep immediately.

Hours later he was awakened by the sound of loud laughing and talking. "Who could that be?" he asked himself. "Perhaps they're a band of thieves. I must hide!" He looked around the room but could see no hiding place. As the voices came closer, he climbed up into the rafters. He was just positioning himself on a beam when the owners of the voices stomped into the room below.

He peered down carefully. He was so shocked he almost fell off the beam. There were several horned goblins which he knew at once must be the *tokkaebis* of which he had heard about all his life.

The *tokkaebis* sat and talked for a short time, each relating what kind of tricks he had played on humans that day. Then they began to sing and dance, laughing boisterously all the while. Every now and then they banged their clubs on the floor and chanted, "Thump! Thump! Come out gold! Thump! Thump! Come out silver!" and gold and silver coins poured out of the clubs.

"I'm thirsty," said one of them.

"Then let's have some wine!" shouted the others in unison.

"Thump! Thump! Come out wine! Thump! Thump! Come

out wine!" they all chanted and several jugs of wine appeared. They drank the wine and called forth more. Then one of them suggested they have some food. "Thump! Thump! Come out rice! Thump! Thump! Come out meat!" They banged their clubs over and over until there was an elaborate meal before them.

Younger Brother became very hungry watching the tokkaebis eat. Then he remembered the hazelnuts in his pocket. He put one in his mouth and bit down hard. "Cuuraack!"

"What was that?" asked one of the tokkaebis.

"The roof is falling!" cried another.

"Let's get out of here!" they all shouted at once and rushed out the door.

Younger Brother was also frightened. He lay where he was until sunup. Then he climbed down from the rafters and looked around inside and outside the house to make sure the tokkaebis were gone.

"Am I hungry!" he said, sitting down to the feast the tokkaebis left. After eating his fill, he gathered up the gold and silver coins scattered all over the floor and found one of the tokkaebi's clubs standing in a corner of the room. "I wonder," he said, smiling. Bang! He hit the floor with the club and said, "Thump! Thump! Come out gold!" and gold coins immediately rattled out. "Thump! Thump! Come out clothes!" he said, and a set of clothes appeared. "Thump! Thump! Come out rice!" he said, and rice appeared.

Younger Brother hurried home to his worried parents. They rejoiced at their good fortune. He bought some land with the gold and silver coins and built a fine house. He used the club to provide whatever food, clothes and other necessities he and his parents needed.

It wasn't long before Older Brother heard that his brother had become wealthy overnight and decided he should go see for himself. When he heard about the tokkaebi's club,

he decided that he had to have one, too. So the next day he set out for the shack in the forest. He stopped to rest under the hazelnut tree and daydreamed about how rich he was going to be when he got a *tokkaebi's* club. He collected some nuts for his parents and his wife and children but then ate them himself. When the sun started getting low, he put a few nuts in his pocket and headed for the shack. He found it with no problem and went inside and climbed up into the rafters to wait for the *tokkaebis* to come. Just when he decided they were not coming, he heard loud laughter.

They came noisily into the house and sat down. They talked about their day's activities and then began playing games with their clubs. Older Brother became so excited at seeing gold and silver coins pour out of the clubs that he took out a hazelnut and crunched down on it with his teeth.

The *tokkaebis* stopped dancing.

"Did you hear that?" asked one.

"Yea," said the others.

"It must be that guy who tricked us last time and made off with my club," said another with a scowl on his face.

"Let's get him!" shouted the others.

The *tokkaebis* began searching the place. Older Brother was so scared his teeth began to chatter.

"There he is," one of them shouted, pointing to the ceiling. "Get him!"

In the blink of an eye, Older Brother found himself on the floor. "No, no. Don't hurt me. Please let me go. Please," he cried, rubbing his hands together.

But the *tokkaebis* just laughed. "Thump! Thump! Beat him up! Beat the thief who stole our club!" they chanted and banged their clubs on the floor. All night they toyed with Older Brother, over and over tickling him, beating him and stretching and shrinking his ears, arms, legs, neck and nose. At the crack of dawn, they disappeared into the forest.

Older Brother finally managed to stand up but he fell over immediately because his nose was so long he could not balance. After several attempts, he succeeded in balancing himself by supporting his nose with his hands. He tried to sneak home but many a villager saw him.

When word of what happened to his brother reached Younger Brother, he took his club and went to his brother's house. "Thump! Thump! Go back in! Make his nose short again!" he said, banging the club on the floor and Older Brother's nose was the size it had been.

"Thank you, thank you," cried Older Brother. "Please forgive me for all the bad things I have done. I want to be good and kind like you. I want to be a good brother and a good son." And from then on, he was.

The Salt Peddler and the Shinbone Ghost

Once upon a time a salt peddler stopped to rest at the foot of a mountain pass. He was weary and his legs and back hurt from carrying his heavy load from one secluded village after another. Carefully he propped his A-frame carrier on the ground and slipped his arms out of the shoulder straps. He sat down with his back against a tree and was soon dozing.

After a while he awoke and glanced around. Something on the ground nearby caught his eye. It looked like a human bone. The thought sent tingles up and down his spine. But his curiosity overcame his fright so he picked it up for a closer look.

"This is just like my shin bone," he muttered to himself and put it back on the ground.

He rested a while longer and then put his A-frame on and left. Hearing something behind him, he looked back and was frightened to see the bone standing in the path. He walked faster, thinking it couldn't go fast. But it went fast as well. Then he slowed down to let it go past. But it also slowed down. Then he stopped, thinking it would go on by. But it also stopped. He didn't know what to do.

At sundown he stopped at a tavern to spend the night. The bone followed him into his room and when he lay down to sleep, it lay down as well. The next morning, it got up when he got up and followed him out the tavern.

This went on for several days. Then one afternoon when they came to the top of a ridge, the peddler noticed that a house in the village below seemed to be having a party.

When they came near the village entrance, he told the bone, "There's a feast at one of the houses. You wait here with the salt while I go get us some meat and rice cakes and wine." He quickly removed his A-frame and walked toward the village. He looked back after a few steps and was delighted to see that the bone had not moved. He went into the village and left by another route.

Several years later when he found himself in the vicinity of that village, he was reminded of the bone and decided to visit the spot where he had last seen it. He went there but there was no trace of it, only the rotten remains of his old A-frame carrier.

He looked around and saw a small tavern that had not been there before. Since it was already late afternoon, he went there and asked to stay the night. The old woman who ran the place took one look at him and said he could.

"Here, have some wine," the old woman said, after he finished his meal. "You must be bored. How about telling me something interesting. Being a peddler, you must have lots of stories."

"Not really. But you must have heard lots of interesting things yourself. You tell me something."

The old woman talked for a while and then she said, "Why don't you have anything to say? Going from place to place you must have seen and heard all kinds of interesting things. And you must have had all kinds of interesting experiences."

"Well, just the other day I was thinking of something that happened to me. You see, I had been going from village to village selling salt and, being very tired, I stopped at the bottom of a pass to rest. I was leaning against a big rock when I noticed something that looked like a bone. I looked at it and said to myself, 'This looks like my shin bone.' And after that, that damn bone made every move I made."

"Well?" said the old woman.

"Well, I was scared. If I walked fast, it walked fast. If I went slow, it went slow. If I stopped, it stopped. The damn thing just kept following me," the peddler took a drink and was quiet.

"Well, what happened?" asked the old woman excitedly.

"I just couldn't shake that damn thing. That night when I went into a tavern to sleep, it lay right down beside me. And the next morning when I headed out, it was right behind me. It followed me for I don't know how many days." He drank down a bowl of wine.

"So, what did you do?"

"Well, one day I happened to come upon a village where some kind of celebration was going on. It was the village just down the road from here. So I said to that bone to wait here with the salt and I would go down and get us some food and drink. I headed down the road but the bone didn't follow. I was so happy to be free of that damn thing. I left that village by a different route and went straight home. That was quite a few years ago. Then, just the other day I found myself near here and, remembering that bone, I came here to see what had become of it. But it was gone. I wonder what became of it."

"I'm that bone!" shouted the old woman and slammed into the peddler.

You Can't Trust a Woman

Once upon a time in a certain village there lived a middle-aged widow. She lived alone because she had no children, her husband having died shortly after her marriage. Although she and her husband had come from good families, she lived a rather hard life.

One day as she was bemoaning her fate, she said to herself, "If only I had a *tokkaebi's* mallet, I could be wealthy." Then she recalled having heard that *tokkaebi* goblins like buckwheat jelly more than anything. "I'll put out some buckwheat jelly to try to befriend a *tokkaebi*."

Unfortunately, it wasn't buckwheat season so she couldn't find any on market day and none of her neighbors had any. She had no choice but to wait until it was harvest time. Anxiously she awaited the harvest, planning and replanning how she would befriend a *tokkaebi*.

At long last, autumn arrived and the harvest began. She bought a lot of buckwheat, so much that her neighbors joked that she was going to live on buckwheat instead of rice. Happily she set about making buckwheat jelly, imagining the day when she would be wealthy.

She could hardly wait for nightfall. At sundown, she cut a large block of the jelly and put it on a lovely dish just outside the gate to her house. The next morning she was delighted to see that it was gone.

That night she put a dish of it just inside the gate and

the next morning it was gone. Then she put a dish of it in the yard a few steps from her door. All night she kept vigil, peeking through a hole in the papered door. Finally, she saw an ugly man-like creature with horns appear, gobble up the buckwheat jelly, and disappear.

The following night she prepared a lavish table of food and placed a dish of buckwheat jelly right outside her door. Again she kept vigil. Around midnight she saw the *tokkaebi* appear and eat the buckwheat jelly. Just as he was taking the last bite, she called out, "Please come in and eat some more."

The *tokkaebi* was hesitant but the thought of more buckwheat jelly was too enticing.

"Don't be shy. I have a lot of buckwheat jelly and a lot of other things, too," the widow called out. "Please, I'm just a lonely woman with no one to share my meals with. Please join me," she pleaded and slowly opened the door.

The *tokkaebi* took a few steps backward. "Please don't go," said the widow. "I have plenty of food. Really I do. Please stay and eat with me."

The *tokkaebi* eyed the woman for a while and then very slowly walked to the door, looked inside at the table laden with food and went into the room.

"Please sit down," said the widow, trying hard not to show her excitement. "I'm glad to have someone to share my meal."

The *tokkaebi* looked nervously around the room and then sat down at the table.

"Please sit comfortably," said the widow. "And please eat a lot. It's not much, but I hope it is to your liking."

Without a word, the *tokkaebi* began to eat with great relish. While he ate, the widow told him all about herself and her difficult life. He never said a word or gave any indication that he understood. When he finished eating, he belched loudly and stood up and adjusted his belt. Then he smiled at the widow and turned toward the door.

"Please come again tomorrow," said the widow.

The *tokkaebi* went out the door and disappeared without a word. The widow was ecstatic. She could hardly sleep the rest of the night.

The next night she prepared another elaborate meal including, of course, a very big dish of buckwheat jelly. She waited anxiously and around midnight the *tokkaebi* appeared with a tap at her door.

Again, the *tokkaebi* ate without a word while the widow chatted incessantly about all kinds of things. When he finished, he moved a little away from the table and took a small silk pouch from his pocket. "You've been very kind to me," he said in a deep, husky voice. "Please take this. I want you to have it," he said, placing the pouch on the table in front of the widow.

"Oh, but I couldn't," the widow said in a humble voice, although she wanted to grab it up and look inside.

"Don't be shy," said the *tokkaebi*. "It is just a little token of my appreciation. Besides I can always get more."

"Thank you, you're very kind," said the widow. "Can you come back tomorrow?"

"No, I can't come tomorrow. But I will visit you in three days," said the *tokkaebi*, and he went out the door.

The widow was so excited she could hardly open the pouch. When she finally got it untied, jewels and coins spilled out. She laughed hysterically as she examined each one.

The widow anxiously awaited the *tokkaebi's* next visit. She worried the whole time whether he would come as promised or not.

But the *tokkaebi* kept his promise. And, to the widow's surprise, he chatted about all kinds of things. He entertained her with stories about his various exploits, including good deeds he had done for some people and bad tricks he had played on others. When he was ready to leave, he presented her with a bigger pouch than before and said that he would come back on a certain day.

Thus the widow and the *tokkaebi* became friends. The *tokkaebi* made regular visits to the widow and always gave her a nice gift. The widow couldn't believe her good fortune and didn't give any thought to asking for its magic mallet.

After a while, she was very wealthy and did not want for anything. She became tired of entertaining the *tokkaebi* and wished that she could make him stop visiting. But she did not know how to make him stop and she was also afraid of him and what he might do.

Then one night when the *tokkaebi* was visiting she said, "You and your kind seem to be very brave. I don't guess there is anything that you are afraid of."

"Oh, I wouldn't say that. We *tokkaebis* don't like horse heads and blood. We're really frightened of them. Nothing will make me go near them."

The day of the *tokkaebi's* next visit, the widow killed a horse and put its head outside the gate. Then she smeared its blood on the outside of the gate and, as an added precaution, on the inside as well. Quietly she kept vigil.

"Ugh! A horse head!" a shout broke the stillness around midnight. And the *tokkaebi* hurried away grumbling to himself, "You can't trust a woman!"

The Fox Girl

T here was once a prosperous stable beside a certain mountain pass. It was run by a couple who had two children, a son and a daughter.

One spring day the daughter went up the mountain behind the house to gather herbs and mushrooms, a task she often did and enjoyed. However, at sundown, she had not returned. The father and son organized the stablemen and headed up the trail to search for her. Just as they reached the top of the first ridge, they saw her coming up the other side.

"What do you mean staying out so late?" stormed the anxious father.

"I'm sorry, Father. I was so tired from walking so much and picking so many herbs that I fell asleep," explained the daughter. "Please don't be angry."

"You should be more careful. A wild animal could have gotten you," said the father. "Next time, don't go so far. It's dangerous."

The next morning one of the horses was found dead in the stable. Everyone was shocked because the horse had shown no signs of illness and decided that it must have died from old age. However, they began to worry when another horse was found dead the following morning and decided to post a guard in the stable that night. The next morning the guard was found dead. The remaining stablemen ran

away because they were afraid of being ordered to guard
the stable.

That night the father told the son to guard the stable.
He hid in some hay and made a peephole so he could see
out. He listened to the sounds of the nearby forest which
he could easily identify.

Then, in the middle of the night, he heard something
which made his spine tingle. It was footsteps. Carefully he
peeped out. He almost shouted for joy when he saw it was
his sister. She stopped a few steps from the stable and put
a bottle of sesame oil on the ground.

Curiously the boy watched her roll up her sleeves and
rub her hands and forearms with sesame oil. Then, to his
horror, she stuck her arm into a horse's anus, pulled out
its liver, and ate it. The boy was petrified. He dared not
move until she went into the house.

At sunup he went inside the house and told his parents
to come out to the stable. He showed them the dead horse
and told them exactly what he had seen during the night.

"Nonsense!" said the father. "You must have been dreaming. And since you apparently fell asleep, you'll guard again tonight."

"But Father, you must believe me. I didn't fall asleep. I promise you. I saw her with my own eyes," said the boy, wringing his hands.

"How dare you accuse your sister of such things!" said the mother.

"But it's true. You must believe me. Something must be..."

"Shut up!" stormed the father. "I've heard enough of your foolish talk. Now get to work. We've got to get rid of this dead horse."

"But Father, please listen to me. Please. I wish it wasn't true but it is. You must believe...."

"Get out! Get out of my sight!" shouted the father as the mother covered her face with her hands and cried.

The boy haplessly walked away as his enraged father swore at him. Not knowing what to do nor where to go, he took the first path that led off the road. He walked until dark and then lay down to sleep under a large tree beside the path.

For several days he wandered aimlessly, begging food at houses along the way. Then one day he saw an old monk trying to cross a swiftly flowing stream. He helped him cross and in return for his kindness the monk invited him to stay at his temple for the night.

After the evening meal, the old monk chatted with the boy. Finally, the boy told him about the tragedy that had befallen his family.

The old monk nodded his head knowingly. "Your sister must have been eaten by a fox which then metamorphosed into her form. It is the fox that you saw."

"Then I must go home," exclaimed the boy, jumping to his feet. "I must warn my parents."

"Wait. I will help you. But I must think about what should be done," said the old monk. "Go to sleep now so you can set out early in the morning."

The next morning the monk told the boy what he should do and gave him three small bottles—a red one, a yellow one and a blue one. "Take this horse," he said, handing him the reins to a white horse. "You must hurry. I fear you are already too late." The boy thanked him and rode off at a gallop.

A couple of days later the boy arrived home. He tied the horse outside the gate and went in cautiously. All was quiet. He tiptoed into the house and found everything in disarray. He went into the yard and came face to face with the fox girl.

"Oh, Brother, you've come home. Where have you been? I've missed you," she said, grabbing his hand in an iron-like grip.

"Where are Mother and Father?" asked the boy, trying to be natural in spite of his fear.

"There was an accident. They're in their graves," she replied coldly and squeezed his hand tighter.

Slowly they walked into the house and sat down. All the while the boy tried to think of a way to escape. Suddenly he said, "Could you prepare some food for me? I'm very hungry."

"All right. But you mustn't run away while I'm in the kitchen. Here, I'm going to tie this to your ankle to make sure you don't," said the fox girl, tying a long piece of string to him which she took from his mother's sewing basket. She smiled broadly and went into the kitchen, trailing the string behind her.

The boy sat quietly trying to think of a way to escape while every few seconds the fox girl pulled on the string to make sure he was there. Finally he untied the string, tied it to the leg of a chest, sneaked out to his horse and galloped away.

"Stop! Stop!" yelled the fox girl as she rushed out of the kitchen. With the speed of a fox, she raced after the boy.

The boy looked back and saw the fox girl grabbing at the horse's tail. Quickly he took out the red bottle and threw it at her. It burst into flames but she managed to escape, although her hair and clothes were badly singed.

She raced after the boy again and soon grabbed hold of the horse's tail. The boy threw the yellow bottle at her. It broke on the ground and a wall of brambles appeared. Although cut and scratched by the thorns, the fox girl managed to get through and was soon grabbing at the horse's tail again.

The boy looked at the last bottle and, praying that it would work, threw it at the fox girl. It broke and a large lake formed before his eyes. He watched the fox girl struggle in the water and sink. Then, to his relief, the dead body of a fox with nine tails floated to the surface.

The Wayfarer, the Foxes and the Tiger

O nce a very long time ago, a wayfarer lost his way in the mountains. He wandered here and there in search of a path but only found himeslf deeper and deeper in a thick forest with nightfall fast approaching. At long last he saw a light in the distance and, thinking it must be a woodsman's house, made his way to it.

He called out from the edge of the glen and, to his surprise, a lovely young woman came out of the house and asked what he wanted.

"This isn't a tavern, but I'll let you stay the night," she said and showed him to a room. "You must be hungry. I'll bring you some food," she said and left.

After eating the wayfarer lay down to sleep. But, despite his tiredness, sleep wouldn't come. He thought about this and that and soon he bagan to wonder about the young woman who appeared to be living alone. Then he became aware of a familiar sound. It gave him an eerie feeling for it was the sound of a knife being sharpened.

Quietly he got to his knees and peeped outside through a hole in one of the room's papered doors. The young woman was sharpening a very large knife. To the wayfarer's horror, her face was not sweet and lovely as before but hard and sinister. Noiselessly he crept out the back door and into the forest. Hidden behind a tree, he watched her go into his room and then rush out and look all around the yard.

Thinking that she intended to kill him and take his money, he clambered up the mountain.

He ran for a while and then, thinking he was safe, stopped to rest. He heard something crack behind him and looked around just in time to see the woman coming after him with the knife. He threw his pack at her and ran away. He ran through bushes and brambles, tearing his clothes and scratching his face and hands. Hurt and exhausted he slumped down behind a large rock to catch his breath.

Suddenly he heard music coming from a distance. The thought of other people revived him and he ran in the direction from which the music came. He found himself on the top of a ridge near a tower from which the music was coming.

"Help me! Help me!" he cried, running toward the tower. "Save me! Please, save me!" he cried and slumped down on the ground at the feet of a bearded man who came out of the tower.

"Help you!" laughed the bearded man, jerking the wayfarer up by the collar and pushing him into the arms of another man. "You're the very bastard who duped my mother! And you're going to die for it! Lock him up!"

The wayfarer was shoved into a small dark room and the door locked. He thought about what was happening and wondered what kind of people the woman and the men were. He wondered if they were ghosts.

He looked through a crack in the door and saw the bearded man coming toward the door with a big knife. Then he noticed a bushy tail trailing behind him.

"A fox!" he exclaimed to himself. "A fox in the form of a man! Oh my god, what shall I do!"

The fox man opened the door and looked at the wayfarer with an evil grin.

"Please, Sir, I don't know why you want to kill me, but

could I ask just one thing?" pleaded the wayfarer.

"What's that?" laughed the fox man.

"Please give me a big jar of water. A very big one so I can quench my thirst before I die."

The fox man brought a very large jar of water. "You asked for a big jar and now you've got it. But be sure to drink every drop," he said with an evil laugh as he closed the door.

Quickly the wayfarer began pouring the water on the adobe wall of the room. He scratched at the wall and poured water on it until he made a hole large enough to crawl through. Unbeknownst to him, the tower stood on the edge of a cliff. He fell over the edge and landed right on a tiger resting at the foot of the cliff.

The tiger dragged the semi-conscious wayfarer to its den in a nearby cave. There she scratched his face and body so that her cubs could feed on his blood and left. When the man came to his senses he killed the cubs with a big stone, left the cave and, not having the strength to go farther, climbed up a nearby tree.

The foxes, in the meantime, tracked the tiger and the wayfarer to the cave. From his perch high up in the tree, the wayfarer watched the foxes go into the cave. And then, just as they came out, the tiger returned.

The tiger attacked at once. She fought viciously and, though outnumbered, killed the foxes. She sniffed at their torn bodies and then fell over dead.

After a while the wayfarer climbed down from the tree and, thinking there was no longer anything to fear, returned to the foxes' house. He rummaged through it and found a large stash of gold and precious jewels. He wrapped the stash with a large cloth and then lay down and slept peacefully.

The next morning he happily put the bundle on his back and left the foxes' house a rich man.

The Fortuneteller and the Demons

L ong, long ago in Hanyang* there lived an unusually gifted fortuneteller who was blind. Although he could not see the world around him, he had the power to see evil spirits.

One day as he was walking down a street he saw a crowd of colorfully dressed demons following several errand boys who were carrying fruit, rice cakes and wine. Thinking that the demons would cause trouble for the household to which the errand boys were bound, the fortuneteller followed at a safe distance. Shortly they went into a nobleman's house.

The fortuneteller waited anxiously outside the gate, trying to fathom what kind of havoc the demons would cause. After a while he heard a scream, followed by loud wailing, coming from the house.

"What's wrong? What's happened?" he asked an errand boy who came out the gate.

"The master's daughter suddenly died," replied the boy, hurrying off down the road.

The fortuneteller called to the gate guard, "Please take me to your master. I'm a fortuneteller. I know what happened to his daughter and I think I can save her. Please, I implore you. Take me to your master. We must hurry

---

* Hanyang: today's Seoul, it was the capital of the Chosŏn Kingdom (1392-1910).

if she is to return to life."

The guard hesitated at first but the fortuneteller was so excited and seemed so sure of himself that he finally told him that he would speak to his master.

The nobleman came out to the gate and the fortuneteller explained what he had observed.

"So what you're saying is that you can revive my daughter?" said the nobleman.

"Yes, but we must hurry. Time is of the essence." The nobleman eyed the fortuneteller and then led him into the house.

The fortuneteller asked that the body of the girl be placed in a small room. Then he closed all the doors and windows tightly and pasted paper over every crack and crevice so that not even smoke could pass through. He sat down beside the body and began to chant.

Presently loud groaning sounds filled the room. But the

fortuneteller continued to chant. The groaning became louder and louder as the demons struggled to get out. Just when it seemed the room would explode with the noise, a curious servant girl made a small hole in the papered window so that she could peep inside. The demons immediately rushed out through the tiny hole.

The dead girl opened her eyes and looked around in a daze. The fortuneteller called in her parents who were overcome with joy.

The fortuneteller refused all the gifts the nobleman offered him. "I don't have long to live. I could have destroyed those demons if someone hadn't made a hole in the window. Now they will surely destroy me."

News of the fortuneteller's uncanny vision which enabled him to bring the nobleman's daughter back to life soon spread throughout the city, even to the King.

The King was very skeptical by nature. He thought that the fortuneteller might be a trickster who could easily take advantage of others, especially ignorant commoners. He decided to summon him to his Court so that he could judge him himself.

The King talked to the fortuneteller for a while and then decided to give him a test. He had a dead rat placed in front of him. "What is on the floor in front of you?" asked the King.

"A rat, Your Majesty," replied the fortuneteller.

The King was surprised. "Can you tell me how many?"

"Yes, Your Majesty. There are three rats," replied the fortuneteller very confidently.

"Three? Did you say three?" laughed the King.

"Yes, Your Majesty. I clearly discern three."

"You fool! There is only one!" stormed the King. "You have no special powers. You're nothing but a charlatan who preys on ignorant, innocent people. And you'll pay with your life...."

"But, Your Majesty, I can see them. Three..."

"You will be publicly beheaded to show the people what becomes of people who practice deceit," said the King sternly and he motioned to some guards to take the fortuneteller out.

Some curious courtiers examined the rat and found two perfectly formed fetuses inside it. They showed them to the King.

"I've made a grave mistake," said the King. "Hurry to the tower and signal that the execution is cancelled," he ordered a guard.

The guard rushed to the tower. He tried to wave the flag to the right to signal the executioners that the man was to be spared. But a strong wind blew it to the left every time he tried.

The fortuneteller was thus beheaded. As his head dropped, evil laughter broke the silence at the execution site and the wind immediately ceased.

Supernatural Spouses

The Snail Lady

T here was a young bachelor who lived all alone. He worked very hard even though he had no one to provide for but himself.

One day while he was working he mumbled to himself, "I don't know why I'm hoeing this field to plant rice when there isn't anyone with whom to eat it."

"You can eat it with me," came a woman's voice from nowhere.

The young man looked around but there was no one. "I must be hearing things," he told himself and started hoeing again.

"*Aigo!* From morning till night I work this field to grow rice but who is there to eat it with?" the young man muttered to himself after a while.

"I'll eat it with you," came the woman's voice again.

"Who said that?" shouted the young man, spinning around in the direction from which the voice came. But again, there was no one. "I really must be hearing things," he said, shaking his head.

"Take me to live with you," came the voice from nearby.

The young man looked all around and then down at his feet. A snail caught his eye. It was unusually large and very pretty. Without thinking he picked it up and put it into his pocket.

That night, when he changed his clothes, the snail fell

out of his pocket. He picked it up and admired its pretty shell. Then he put it in the water jar in the kitchen.

The next morning when he woke up, the young man was shocked to find dishes of hot food on his table. He ate the food, all the while wondering who could have prepared it.

That night, when he returned home, he found another table of hot food. Happily he ate it, thinking it was the best food he had ever eaten and how wonderful it would be to have a wife who could prepare delicious foods for him all the time. "Tomorrow I must find out who made this food for me. I must," he told himself.

The next morning he ate and then left the house as he usually did, taking his farm tools with him. But he didn't go far. He quickly hid his tools behind a nearby tree and returned home. Quietly he peeked into the kitchen.

He couldn't believe his eyes. A beautiful young woman was climbing out of the water jar. She stretched her arms and straightened her dress and then started cleaning the kitchen. All day the young man secretly watched her clean the house and wash and mend his clothes. When the sun began to set, she prepared dinner and then got back inside the water jar.

As he ate dinner, the young man could not help thinking how wonderful it would be to have her for a wife. He decided to try to catch her.

The next morning he pretended to go out to work and then he slipped into the kitchen and waited beside the water jar for the woman to come out.

When the woman finally came out, the young man grabbed her and said, "Please be my wife."

The woman's cheeks flushed and she nodded her head in consent.

They lived very happily as husband and wife. But then one day the King came to their area to hunt.

As the King rode past their house on horseback, he saw them working in the yard. "How can a beautiful woman like her be the wife of a dirt farmer?" he exclaimed. "I'll have to take her for my wife."

The King ordered his men to set up camp and ordered the young man brought to him.

"I want to have a contest," the King told the young man. "See that mountain," he said, pointing to one nearby, "let's see which of us can cut down the most trees on it the fastest. If I lose, I will give you half of my kingdom. If you lose, you must give me your wife."

"Don't worry," said the snail lady when the young man told her what the King proposed. She wrote something on a piece of paper and then tied it to a ring she took off her finger. "Take this and throw it into the sea," she said, handing him the letter and ring. "Then my father, the Dragon King, will help you."

The young man did as he was told and at once the sea parted, revealing a long road leading downward. He followed the road to the Dragon King's palace. The Dragon King gave him a gourd and sent him home.

On the day of the contest the King brought hundreds of soldiers to cut the trees. The young man cut open the gourd from the Dragon King and out came an endless stream of tiny men with axes and they began felling trees right and left. Needless to say the young man won the contest to the dismay of everyone, especially the King.

But the King did not keep his promise. Instead he challenged the young man to be the first to cross the river on horseback. Once again the snail lady sent the young man to her father. The Dragon King gave him a small, skinny horse which looked like it would collapse any minute. However, it ran like the wind, leaving the King and his large steed far behind.

The King was furious. Instead of keeping his promise, he called for a boat race. The Dragon King gave the young man a very small boat. It looked no bigger than a hand beside the King's large, dazzling one. However, it shot ahead of the King's boat like an arrow. The King jumped up and down in frustration. Then all at once a huge wave appeared and swallowed up his boat.

The young man gave all of the King's belongings to the poor and he and the snail lady lived happily ever after.

The Woodcutter and the Heavenly Maiden

O nce upon a time a handsome young woodcutter lived with his mother at the foot of the Diamond Mountains. He was very diligent and every day he went into the forest to cut firewood to sell to his neighbors. Still, he was so poor he couldn't afford to marry. However, he never complained about his situation, even though he longed very much to have a wife.

One day when he was working in the forest, the woodcutter heard something running. He stopped chopping and looked around. He was surprised to see a deer running toward him.

"Help! Help! Please help me!" cried the deer. "There's a hunter after me. Please don't let him kill me."

Quickly the woodcutter hid the deer under some limbs which he had cut from the trees he had chopped down. Then he started chopping a tree but, before he could swing his axe a third time, the hunter appeared.

"Did a deer run by here?" asked the hunter.

"Yes," replied the woodcutter, "it ran down into that valley."

"Thanks," shouted the burly hunter as he rushed off in the direction the woodcutter pointed, a bow in one hand and an arrow in the other.

The deer crawled out from under the tree limbs and thanked the woodcutter. "You saved my life. To repay your kindness, I will help you fulfill your fondest wish. I can do it because I am a servant of *Sanshin*.*

"Listen carefully. Tonight the moon will be full. When the moon comes up, climb to the top of that mountain. There is a lake there where maidens from heaven come to bathe. While they are bathing, hide the clothes of one of them. Without her clothes, she will not be able to return to heaven. She will become your wife. But it is very important that you do not give her clothes back until you have four children. You must not forget that." With those words, the deer ran up the mountain slope.

The woodcutter did not know whether to believe the deer or not. But that night he climbed to the top of the mountain and hid in some shrubs on a small cliff overlooking the lake. Soon a group of the most beautiful maidens he had ever seen came floating down through the moonlit mist. They chatted merrily as they disrobed and hung their clothes on tree branches and jumped into the lake.

The spellbound woodcutter stared at the maidens as they frolicked in the water. After a while he came to his senses and remembered the deer's instructions. Stealthily he crept to the trees where the maiden's clothes were hanging and took the prettiest set. He carefully folded the filmy garments and put them inside his jacket. Then he hid and watched the maidens play in the water.

When the moonlight began to dim the maidens came out of the water and each went to where she had hung her clothes.

"Oh no. Where are my clothes? I can't find my clothes," cried the youngest maiden.

They searched here and there for the clothes but to no avail. Time was running out for they had to return before

---

Sanshin: the Mountain Spirit, a Shamanist inspired god.

the closing of the Heavenly Gates. Finally, they floated up into the sky, leaving the youngest one behind.

Utterly bewildered, the maiden slumped down on the ground and cried.

Quietly, the woodcutter approached her. "Don't cry," he said in a soft voice. "Everything will be all right. You can come live at my house." He apologized over and over for causing her so much trouble and begged her to forgive him. He seemed so sincere and gentle that she finally agreed to go home with him.

At first the heavenly maiden found life on earth confusing but soon she became accustomed to the domestic routine and found it much to her liking. The months passed and she gave birth to a son. With time she gave birth to two more children. She was very happy and content taking care of her husband, children, and mother-in-law.

Then one day she began to think about her family and friends in heaven and wished she could see them. That evening, when the woodcutter came home from the forest, she said, "My dear husband, I haven't seen my heavenly clothes in a very long time. Won't you please show them to me? I just want to see them and touch them."

The woodcutter felt sorry for having kept the clothes hidden from her. Disregarding the deer's advice, he brought the clothes out for her to see.

"Oh, they are so beautiful," she said fondling them. She quickly put them on and at once was overcome by a desire to return to heaven. She grabbed the children and, before the woodcutter realized what was happening, began to float up to heaven with a child under each arm and one between her legs.

"Come back! Come back!" screamed the woodcutter, "Don't leave me! Come back!" But his wife floated higher and higher until he could no longer see her.

The woodcutter was overcome with grief. He reproached himself for not following the deer's instructions. Every day he went into the forest to cut wood but instead of chopping trees, he always ended up gazing up at heaven and longing for his wife and children.

One day when he was sitting in the forest, gazing up at heaven, the deer which he saved appeared. He was very happy to see the deer and told it all that had happened.

"You didn't follow my instructions," said the deer, "but I'll help you because you saved my life that time. Go to the lake at the top of the mountain tonight. You will see a golden bucket come down from heaven. Ever since you took the clothes, the maidens do not go there to bathe. Instead, they lower a golden bucket and draw water up to heaven from the lake. Get inside the bucket and you will be pulled up to heaven. That is the only way you will be able to see your wife and children." With those words, the deer ran off toward a stream.

That evening the woodcutter climbed up the mountain to the lake and waited for the golden bucket to come down from heaven. When it finally came down, he quickly climbed in and was pulled up to heaven.

Upon his arrival in heaven, the maidens took him to the palace to see the King of the Heavenly Kingdom. There he met his wife and children for she was the King's daughter. The King gave him permission to stay in heaven with his family.

The woodcutter quickly adjusted to life in heaven. He and his family were very happy. They had beautiful clothes to wear and delicious food to eat every day. The woodcutter had no worries. But he often thought about his mother who was very old and living all alone on earth.

One day he told his wife that he missed his mother very much and wanted to go see her. The heavenly maiden understood how he felt for she also missed her mother-in-law very much. She told him that she didn't think there was a way for him to visit his mother and return to heaven but that she would go ask her father.

Presently she returned and told the woodcutter, "Father has arranged for a winged-horse to take you to earth to visit your mother. When you arrive you must not dismount, for if your feet touch the ground you will not be able to return to heaven, not ever."

The woodcutter mounted the winged-horse and in an instant they were at his mother's house. "Mother, Mother, come quick!" he shouted and before long he was telling her all about his family and life in heaven and, of course, why he couldn't get off the horse.

When it came time for the woodcutter to return to heaven, his mother said, "Oh, my dear boy, you can't leave without eating something. Let me get you a bowl of pumpkin porridge. It's still your favorite, isn't it?"

A few minutes later she returned from the kitchen with a steaming bowl of pumpkin porridge. With tears in his eyes, the woodcutter took the bowl from his mother. But it was too hot for him to hold so he dropped it, spilling the contents on the neck of the horse. The horse reared up, throwing the woodcutter to the ground, and flew up to heaven.

The woodcutter was grief-stricken. Every day he stood outside, looking up to heaven and calling to his wife and children. At last he died of grief and was transformed into a rooster. That is why roosters crow with their necks stretched upward toward heaven.

Reward and Punishment

Kyŏn-u the Herder and Chik-nyŏ the Weaver

O nce upon a time in a land beyond the stars there lived a lovely princess called Chik-nyŏ. She was the only daughter of the ruler of that land.

Weaving was Chik-nyŏ's favorite pastime. She was very skillful and no one in the land could weave more beautiful or sturdier fabrics than her. That was why she was called Chik-nyŏ, meaning Weaving Maiden.

The King was very proud that Chik-nyŏ was uncommonly diligent and he would often watch her as she worked at her loom. One day when he was watching her weave, he was struck by her beauty. He realized that she was no longer a little girl but a lovely young woman and decided that it was time for her to marry.

He called a meeting of his advisors to consult about eligible bachelors. After several days one of his closest advisors announced that he had found the perfect match for Chik-nyŏ in a neighboring kingdom.

"He's a prince," explained the man. "But he's also a herder. That's why he's called Kyŏn-u. A herder and a weaver, there could not be a better match."

All of the advisors agreed so the King sent a high court official to the neighboring kingdom to try to arrange a marriage between Kyŏn-u and Chik-nyŏ. The neighboring King was delighted with the offer for he had been looking for the perfect wife for his son.

After the Kings' emissaries met several times, a day was selected for the marriage and everyone in the two kingdoms began preparing for the royal wedding. Kyŏn-u and Chik-nyŏ were counselled by their parents about how to behave as man and wife and how to be an exemplary couple.

Finally Kyŏn-u and Chik-nyŏ were married. There was not a happier or more hard working couple anywhere. However, they began to neglect their duties. They were so in love that all they wanted to do was frolic. They would lay in each other's arms and count the stars or run hand-in-hand through the meadows. Chik-nyŏ's loom became dusty and Kyŏn-u's cows wandered about freely, even into the palace flower gardens.

Their subjects began to worry because Chik-nyŏ's father was a stern ruler and did not tolerate idleness. When he heard that Kyŏn-u and Chik-nyŏ were neglecting their work, he was sad and angry. He sent word that they were to appear before him.

"I want you out of my sight. I can't bear to look at the two of you," he said in a stern voice as Kyŏn-u and Chik-nyŏ knelt before him. "You disobeyed your King. I told you to work hard and not neglect your duties and you would always be happy. But you have spent your time together only playing. By being irresponsible, you have set a bad example for your countrymen. Your irresponsibility apparently comes from living together. So you will live apart from now on. Kyŏn-u, you will live in the east and you, Chik-nyŏ, will live in the west."

"Oh, My Lord, My Lord. Please forgive us. We made a mistake," cried Kyŏn-u. "Please don't make us live apart. We'll change. We'll work hard. Please forgive us."

"Oh, Father, please don't make us live apart. I'll do whatever you say but please don't make me live without my husband," pleaded Chik-nyŏ, tears streaming down her face. "I'll work hard at my loom. Please let us live together."

But the King was unmoved. He sent Kyŏn-u to a remote kingdom in the east to tend cows and Chik-nyŏ to a remote kingdom in the west to weave. The two wept so much that the King took pity on them and said they could meet once a year alongside the Silvery River on the seventh day of the seventh moon.

Although he tended his cows, Kyŏn-u could not keep his mind on his work. He passed the time thinking about the blissful days he had spent with Chik-nyŏ, staring at the western heaven where she lived and counting the days until they could be together. Chik-nyŏ spent her days in front of her loom but her eyes were on the eastern heaven where Kyŏn-u lived.

Finally a year passed and it was time for them to meet. With racing hearts, each set out on the long walk to the Silvery River. But they were greatly disappointed when they arrived there for it was so wide that they could hardly see each other or talk. And there was no bridge or boat they could use to cross. They stared at each other across the river and wept.

Kyŏn-u and Chik-nyŏ's tears fell to earth as rain. They cried so much that their tears resulted in floods. Fearing for their lives and homes, the birds and animals on earth came together to decide how to stop the torrents of tears.

"If this rain is to stop," grunted a bear, "Kyŏn-u and Chik-nyŏ must be able to meet face to face."

"That's right," said a rabbit. "But the Silvery River is so vast, how can they get across?"

"There should be a bridge," said an owl. "Let's build one."

"How can we?" roared a tiger. "The Silvery River is too high."

"I know," chirped a magpie. "My fellow magpies and I can do it with the help of our cousins the crows."

"That's a great idea," said a crow. "Let's go!"

The sky became black as all the magpies and crows on earth flew off toward the Silvery River. With their wings spread wide, the birds formed a bridge across the river.

When they realized what the birds had done, Kyŏn-u and Chik-nyŏ stopped crying and rushed to each other across the feathery bridge. They held each other all night and talked about their happy life together and how much they missed each other. As dawn began to break, they shed a few tears and parted to return to their posts in the east and the west.

Since that time, magpies and crows have not been seen on earth on the seventh day of the seventh moon. However, on the next day they can be seen with noticeably less head feathers, no doubt the result of Kyŏn-u and Chik-nyŏ stepping lightly on their heads to cross the Silvery River. There is always a light sprinkling of rain in the early morning of the seventh day of the seventh moon which is the tears Kyŏn-u and Chik-nyŏ shed as they part for another year's separation.

Those in the West know Kyŏn-u and Chik-nyŏ as the bright stars Altair and Vega and the Silvery River as the Milky Way. In the early evening of the seventh day of the seventh moon, the two stars are actually visible directly overhead on each side of the Milky Way.

The Big Dipper Brothers

A very long time ago there were seven brothers who lived with their widowed mother in a small house in a valley at the foot of a mountain. Although they had known only poverty, they were all very happy and very devoted to their mother. They worked hard to eke out a living from their meager land and wanted nothing more than their mother to be happy.

But one year, try as they may, they could not seem to make her happy. She always looked sad and tired and they often heard her say to herself, "Oh, I'm cold. So cold!"

"Mother, are you sick? Is something the matter?" they would ask.

"No, no. I'm not sick," she would say, unconsciously pulling her shawl around her. "Don't worry. There's nothing wrong with your old mother."

But the brothers did worry. They made her room even warmer, but still she appeared to be cold. And they tried giving her what delicious meats, fruits and vegetables they could manage to buy or barter, but still she was glum.

Then one day the oldest brother awoke in the middle of the night. He decided to look in on his mother to see if she was sleeping all right but to his dismay her room was empty.

"That's strange. Where could she be?" he wondered aloud and, shaking his head, went back to his room and lay down.

Pretending to be asleep, he waited anxiously for her to return. Just before dawn she returned and went directly into the kitchen and began preparing breakfast.

"Good morning, Mother. How did you sleep?" asked the oldest brother when they all sat down to breakfast.

"Oh, just fine," she said, nodding her head.

"That's good," said the oldest brother with a smile on his face.

That night he went to bed with his brothers as usual but feigned sleep. "I must stay awake. I have to follow her if she goes out," he told himself over and over to keep from falling asleep.

Finally he heard her door slide open and shut and then after a few moments he heard the gate open and close. He was up in an instant and out the gate. He followed ever so quietly and, since the moon was full, was careful to stay far enough behind that his shadow did not spread into her view.

"Where could she be going on such a cold night?" he asked himself as he pulled his coat collar up around his neck.

Soon they came to an icy stream. He was shocked to see her pull up her skirt and wade across. "No wonder she's always cold," he told himself as he waded across. "I'd be cold too if I did this every night."

When she came to a fork in the trail, he was surprised to see which path she took. It led to the house of an old widower who supported himself by weaving straw shoes.

She stood in front of the thatched cottage and straightened her clothes. "Are you home, Old Man? Are you home?" she suddenly called out. Hiding in the shadows, the oldest brother jumped as her scratchy voice sliced the silence.

"Welcome, welcome," said the old man above the screeching of the door. In the candlelight streaming out the open door, the oldest brother saw the old man give his mother a hand to help her step up and then over the threshold into the room.

He crept closer to the house and listened for some time to his mother and the old man talking. He realized that his mother was lonely and needed someone her age with whom to talk. He ran home as fast as he could and woke his brothers and told them what he had seen and heard.

"We must do something for her," said one of the brothers.

"I know," said another, "let's build a bridge over the stream."

"Yes," said the oldest. "That's what we'll do. But we can't tell her we did it. She would be embarrassed to know that we knew about her meetings with the old shoe maker."

"Let's go," said another. "We must hurry to get it done for her return."

The brothers dressed quickly and ran to the stream. Without stopping to catch their breath, they set about placing stepping stones in the water. When they finished, they returned home and went back to bed.

Their mother was very surprised to see the stepping stones. She couldn't imagine who had put them there. She prayed out loud, "Hanŭnim, please bless whoever put these stones here and when they die please make them stars in your heaven."

The woman was very happy the rest of her life and when she died the brothers buried her in a sunny spot on a hill overlooking the stream. The brothers lived long and happy lives and when they died they became stars which together are known as the Big Dipper.

Sun and Moon

Long, long ago a widow lived with her son and daughter in a small isolated house deep in the mountains. Every day she walked several ri* through the forest to the nearest village to work in a nobleman's house. The children played and kept the house while she was away.

One day she did not leave the nobleman's house until after sundown because he held a party. But she did not mind because the nobleman's wife gave her a basket of buckwheat puddings to take to her children.

On her way home, as she came around a bend in the trail, a tiger jumped out from behind some rocks. "What's that you're carrying on your head?" he growled.

"A basket of buckwheat puddings," replied the woman.

"Give me one or I'll eat you up," roared the tiger. So the woman gave him a pudding and he let her pass.

The woman hurried off down the path, thinking how lucky she was. But when she rounded the next bend, there was the tiger, blocking her way.

"That buckwheat pudding was very tasty," said the tiger. "Give me another one or I'll eat you up." The woman gave him one and went on her way.

But the tiger was not content. He stopped her again and again until her basket was empty.

---

*Ri: a measure of distance, about one-third of a mile.

The woman hurried on but soon the tiger jumped out from behind a tree and blocked her way again. "Now what do you want?" yelled the woman. "You ate all my buckwheat puddings." And she threw the basket into the bushes beside the path.

"What are those things swinging at your sides?" growled the tiger.

"They are my arms," said the woman.

"Give me one or I'll eat you up," roared the tiger. So the woman gave him an arm and went on her way.

But the tiger ran ahead and jumped out onto the path again. "I'm still hungry," he roared. "Give me that other arm or I'll eat you up." So the woman gave him her other arm and trudged on down the path.

Around the next bend, the tiger jumped out at her again. "Give me your legs or I'll eat you up," he growled.

"Oh no, no, I can't," said the woman. "I need them to walk home to my children. How will I be able to go home if I give you my legs?"

"You can roll, can't you?" roared the tiger.

So the woman gave him her legs and, rolling over and over, went on her way. But the tiger ran after her and gobbled her up in one gulp.

Back home, the children waited for their mother to return. At nightfall they went inside the house and locked the door as their mother had told them to do. They were very hungry but there was no food so they laid down on their pallets on the floor and waited for their mother to come home.

Meanwhile, the cunning tiger put on the woman's clothes and, as she had done, tied a towel around his head. He walked to her house and, standing erect on his hind legs, tried to open the gate.

"It's Mother! It's Mother!" cried the woman's daughter,

jumping up from her pallet.

"Oh children, it's me. Open the gate," called the tiger.

"Mother, Mother, you're home!" called the little girl, running out the door.

But her brother grabbed her before she got to the gate. "That's not Mother's voice," he said in a loud voice. "Mother has a sweet voice but that..."

"My voice is strange because I had to scream at sparrows all day to keep them away from the barley I spread out on mats to dry," called the tiger, trying to disguise his voice. "Lift the latch, my darlings. I've brought you some buckwheat puddings."

But the children were wary. "Put your arm through the hole in the gate," they said.

The tiger put his arm through the hole and the children felt it. "Why is your arm so rough and hairy?" they asked.

"I had to starch some clothes with rice paste when I did the laundry today. I guess the starch made my hands and arms rough," replied the tiger.

But the children were still not convinced. They peeked out through the hole in the gate and saw that it was a tiger dressed in their mother's clothes. They were very frightened but they were also very clever. "Just a minute," they said, "and we'll let you in." Then, without a sound, they ran behind the house and climbed a big tree near the well and hid in its branches.

After a few moments the tiger called, "Oh children, what are you doing? Open the gate, please." Receiving no reply, he forced open the gate and rushed through the yard and into the house. Roaring loudly, he searched the house for the children. Then he went outside and searched the yard.

Finally, the tiger sat down beside the well to rest. Looking into the water, he saw the boy and girl's reflection. "Oh my, you've fallen into the well. Let me help you out," he said and he tried to pull the children out of the well.

Watching from high up in the tree, the children burst into laughter. The tiger looked up and spotted them among the tree branches.

"Oh, my poor children. Let me help you down," said the tiger and he began to climb the tree. But the tree bark was so slippery he kept sliding down. "How did you get up there?" he shouted at the children.

"We used sesame oil," said the boy. "There's some in the kitchen."

The tiger ran to the kitchen and returned with a jug of sesame oil. He rubbed oil all over the tree trunk and then tried to climb up. He tried again and again but he slipped down every time.

The children could not help laughing at the tiger. "That stupid tiger," the girl suddenly blurted out, "all he has to do is get an axe and cut notches in the tree."

"Hush!" shouted the boy. But it was too late for the tiger had heard her and already was rushing to the house to find an axe. He was back in a few seconds and, cutting notches, climbed up toward the children.

As the tiger came closer and closer, the children began to pray. "Oh Hanŭnim," called out the boy, "don't let the tiger get us. Please save us. Please save us from the tiger."

Immediately a golden chain came down from heaven. The children grabbed hold of it and were quickly pulled up to the Heavenly Kingdom.

Watching the children ascending into the clouds, the tiger prayed, "Oh Hanunim, please pull me up to heaven, too," and immediately a rope came down. He grabbed the rope and was pulled upward to the sky, but, being rotten, the rope broke and the tiger fell to the ground and landed in a buckwheat patch.

The boy and girl lived happily in the Heavenly Kingdom.

But one day the King summoned them to his palace and said, "Children, it is time for you to go to work for no one can be idle here. I have some special tasks for you to perform." So he made the boy the sun and the girl the moon.

But the girl didn't like being the moon because she had to travel during darkness so the boy changed places with her. However, being a modest girl, she was embarrassed when people gazed up at her so she made herself shine brighter and brighter until it became impossible for people to look directly at her.

As for the tiger, his body shattered when he hit the ground and his blood gushed out onto the buckwheat plants. It is said that the roots of buckwheat are red to this day because of his blood.

The Gift from the Mountain Spirit

I n times beyond recall there was a young couple who had a small son whom they loved dearly. They lived with the man's elderly father in a village near a stream.

The grandfather fell ill shortly after his grandson's first birthday. The couple tried all kinds of remedies. The young man traveled far and wide to purchase herbal medicines and his wife brewed them and spooned the tonic into the old man's mouth. They fed him special foods such as snake and carp. They made offerings to Buddha. They tried everything that they heard might cure him, but nothing seemed to help.

Then they began to pray to *Sanshin*, the Mountain Spirit. Every day they prayed to him. Sometimes they went into the nearby forest or up the mountain behind the village to pray to him before large trees or rocks or a spring.

Then one morning the woman said to her husband, "I had a most unusual dream last night."

"That's strange. I, too, had an unusual dream last night. I don't know what to think of it. Anyway, tell me about yours," said the man.

"Well, I dreamed about an old man with long white hair and a long white beard. He carried a staff and a big tiger walked at his side. He said that he lived in the mountain, that he wanted to help us, and that he knew how to cure Grandfather. He said that the only way to cure him was..."

"Let me guess," interrupted the man. "He told you that the only way to cure him was to...to...to kill our boy and make a soup for him to eat."

"That's right. That's exactly what he said. I tried to ask if there was no other way, but he just walked into the forest."

"It was the *Sanshin*. It had to be," said the man. "I had the same dream."

The two were silent for a long time. Finally, the woman said, "What shall we do?"

"We have no choice. We prayed to the *Sanshin*, and he answered our prayers. We can have more children, but we can never have another father." The wife nodded as tears rolled down her cheeks and dropped into her lap.

The two wept for a very long time. Finally, the man got slowly to his feet and went out into the yard. The woman followed. They built a fire and put a large pot of water on it. As the water began to boil loudly, the little boy came out of his grandfather's room where he had been playing.

"What are you cooking?" he asked and skipped around the pot.

The man and woman looked at each other and tears poured down their cheeks. Like a madman, the man grabbed up the boy, dropped him into the pot and slammed on the lid. Then he fell down on the ground and wailed, pounding his fists on the ground. The woman slumped down on the ground and wept.

"Mommy, why are you crying? What's wrong, Mommy? What's wrong with Daddy?" the woman heard a little voice beside her.

She looked in disbelief. It was a boy that looked just like her son. She blinked. He was still there.

"Are you a ghost that's come back to haunt us?" she said.

"That's funny, Mommy. Are you playing a game?" asked the boy and he began to shout, "Daddy, Daddy, come play with us."

The man raised his head and stared at the boy. Then he got up and walked over to him. He touched his cheek. He squeezed his shoulder. He felt him all over. He picked him up and shouted joyously, "You're alive! You're alive! My son, you're alive!"

The man and woman danced for joy while the boy laughed happily. Suddenly the man became quiet. He put the boy down and looked at the pot. He went over to it and carefully removed the lid. Inside was a very large man-shaped root called ginseng.

That evening the woman fed the ginseng soup to the grandfather. The next morning he was strong enough to feed it to himself. And, by the time he ate the last bowl of it, he was fully recovered.

The man and woman bowed to the mountain to thank the *Sanshin* for the gift he had bestowed on them. He gave it to them because he admired the way they cared for the grandfather and because they were willing to give up something they held dear to save him.

Carp in Winter

In a certain small village a long time ago there lived a young farmer whose surname was Han. He took such good care of his elderly parents that the villagers called him Han Hyoja, *hyoja* meaning filial son.

One cold winter day Han Hyoja tried to encourage his mother, who had been confined to bed for a long time with a debilitating illness, to eat. "Please, Mother, you need to eat something. You should eat to build up your strength."

"I know but I just don't have any appetite," she replied feebly.

Han Hyoja held her bony hand and said, "Mother, if you can think of anything that you might like to eat, or that might stimulate your appetite, just tell me."

"Well...I wonder if there are any carp these days.... Maybe if I ate some carp but..."

On hearing this Han Hyoja quickly left the house to buy a carp. The fish market was on the other side of the river so he boarded a ferry.

When the boat reached the middle of the river, something shiny flipped over the side of the boat and landed on the floor. Han Hyoja and the boatman stared in disbelief. It was a big carp.

"Would you please sell me this fish, Sir?" Han Hyoja asked the boatman. "You see I'm on my way now to buy a carp at the market."

The boatman shook his head back and forth. "No. It's not often that a fish jumps into the boat. I'm going to take this one. I can use it for an offering or the memorial rites. It might bring me luck."

Han Hyoja went to every stall in the market and was told over and over that it was too cold for carp. Empty-handed and with a heavy heart he headed home.

When the ferry reached the middle of the river, something shiny flipped over the side of the boat and landed on the floor. The old boatman looked and blinked. It was another carp.

"That's strange! Really strange!" he mumbled, picking up the big fish. He looked around at the passengers. "What a coincidence," he muttered to himself, seeing Han Hyoja among them. "That guy was on the boat when that other carp jumped inside. How odd that..."

"Hey! You young guy!" he called to Han Hyoja after a while. "Didn't you tell me earlier that you were going to buy a carp?"

"Yes, that's right."

"Why do you want a carp?" asked the boatman.

"Because my sick mother said she would like to eat some."

The boatman stared hard at Han Hyoja's face. "Are you by any chance Han Hyoja?"

"Yes, I'm Han."

The boatman smiled. "Now I understand. Heaven sent the carp to you because you are so devoted to your parents. There's no doubt about it. Heaven sent them. They're your reward for being a filial son." The boatman handed Han Hyoja the two fish. "Here, you take these. You deserve them."

Han Hyoja fed his mother the carp and in no time she recovered from her illness and lived a long and happy life. Needless to say, Han Hyoja also lived a long and happy life.

Rice from Heaven

L ong ago in a certain village there was a young
woman whose husband died shortly after they were
married. She lived with her elderly mother-in-law who
was also a widow. She worked as a day laborer to support
them.

One day she went to work at a neighbor's house. But
it rained so she was unable to complete the work and thus
received no pay. Walking home, she worried about her
mother-in-law because she did not have anything to prepare for her dinner. Tears streamed down her face as she
thought about her poverty and how she was a failure as
a daughter-in-law since she could not take care of her
mother-in-law properly.

She turned down a narrow footpath but stopped short
because there was a pile of dog shit in the way. Carefully
stepping over it, she could not help noticing that it con-
tained a lot of barley. Absentmindedly she watched the rain
wash away the shit until she became aware that she was
looking at a small pile of barley.

Her first thought wasn't that it was dirty but that it was
a waste to have given a bowl of barley to a dog. She suddenly scooped it up into her skirt and hurried home, thinking it would be better to feed her mother-in-law the barley
than let her go hungry.

At home, she washed the barley over and over and put

it on the fire to cook. The steam it emitted had a wonderfully savory smell, but, knowing where the barley had come from, she hesitated to take it in to her mother-in-law when it was ready to serve. She ate a spoonful to make sure nothing was wrong with it and found it surprisingly tasty.

Mother-in-law ate her meal with great relish and wondered how her daughter-in-law had made a simple bowl of barley taste so good.

Daughter-in-law took the dishes into the kitchen to wash. Suddenly there came a loud clap of thunder. It scared her and set her to worrying. She wondered if it was Heaven's way of punishing her for feeding her mother-in-law the barley from dog shit. But she also worried about how she was going to be able to feed her if it continued to rain because she wouldn't be able to find work. Worrying about this, that and the other, she finished cleaning the kitchen and stepped outside to go into the house.

To her surprise, there was a large square box in the middle of the yard. She looked closely and found that it was a rice box she had never seen. "Now that's strange. Who could have left this here? I better take it in out of the rain." It was very heavy but she managed to carry it into the kitchen.

She wiped the rain off the box and opened it. She couldn't believe her eyes. It was full of rice. "Now who in the world could have left this?" she wondered.

It made her happy to think that she did not have to worry, at least for a few days, about where she was going to get the food to feed her mother-in-law. She was so happy that she carried the rice box in to show her.

"I'm sure it must have come from Heaven," said Mother-in-law. "Heaven must have sent it with that big bolt of thunder. It must be your reward for taking such good care of me. You should take good care of it."

"Yes, Mother-in-law, I will," said the young woman. But she thought that it must have come from a neighbor who was trying to help them.

The next morning when she opened the rice box to prepare breakfast she silently thanked whoever had left the box of rice for them. And when she served the rice she couldn't help thinking how thankful she was to be able to serve her mother-in-law some nice rice for a change.

That evening when she went into the kitchen to prepare the evening meal, she again thanked whoever was responsible for their good fortune. She opened the rice box and shook her head. "That's strange, it doesn't look like I took any rice out this morning. I guess the sight of so much rice is too much for my eyes. They must be playing tricks on me." She laughed as she scooped out the rice to prepare dinner.

The next morning she was surprised to find that the box was full. "That's strange," she muttered, taking out enough rice for the morning and midday meals. "Wouldn't it be nice if it stayed full all the time."

That evening she couldn't believe her eyes when she opened the rice box. It was full. "I'll just see what happens if I take out a lot of rice," she muttered to herself and began scooping out the rice.

The next morning she screamed for joy when she opened the box and found it full again. She ran to her mother-in-law. "You were right! You were right! It is a special rice box!" she exclaimed and, amidst tears of joy, told her mother-in-law all about the box. She was so happy that she even told her about the barley from the dog shit.

"That's it! That's it for sure!" said Mother-in-law. "It's a gift from Heaven. A reward for taking such good care of me. You are a wonderful daughter-in-law. There can be none better. And this proves it. Even Heaven was impressed. I could not be happier!" Saying this, Mother-in-law stood up and began to dance around, singing over and over "She's wonderful! She's wonderful! My daughter-in-law is wonderful!"

The two women lived happily ever after.

A Meal of Worms

Along time ago a certain village was struck by a severe drought. The earth cracked and the crops shrivelled on the vines.

Among the hardest hit was an industrious young couple who were known throughout the village for their devotion to the young man's blind mother. As conditions worsened, she became more and more restless and unhappy because she felt that she was a burden to her son and daughter-in-law.

One day she said, "I think I should just die. You have enough to worry about without having to worry about this old sightless hag. I'm tired of being a burden to everyone."

"Now that's no way to talk," said Daughter-in-law. "You're not a burden to anyone."

"Yes, I am. And with times the way they are, you would be better off without having to care for this old woman who can't see a thing."

"Mother, you shouldn't even think such thoughts," said Daughter-in-law. "It's only right that we should take care of you."

"And you must live a long time so you can enjoy your grandchildren," said Son.

"Of course I would like to be able to see my grandchildren. But, with these eyes, that would be impossible. I would just be a burden to them too."

"Now, now, Mother. Don't worry so. When this drought

is over, everything will improve. And you must live until we have children," said Son.

"Oh, if only I could really see them," Mother muttered and became silent.

The young couple worked even harder but, come harvest time, they had nothing to show for their hard work but one sack of rice. The cabbage, the peppers, the garlic, the potatoes, all the crops they needed for winter failed.

"I'll find work elsewhere," Son told his wife. "We have to eat and we will have to buy seeds. It's the only way. I'll bring some food supplies as soon as I can. Please take care of Mother." He then bid farewell to his mother and left home with a heavy heart.

Daughter-in-law gathered herbs and wild vegetables on the mountain to feed Mother. But she couldn't gather a lot because all the other villagers were also gathering them. And she couldn't go far into the mountains because she couldn't leave Mother alone for very long. Within a few days, the nearby slopes were stripped of anything edible.

Daughter-in-law worried about Mother's health and how she could continue to feed her. Crouching in a corner of the kitchen, she scratched at the earthen floor as she thought. Finally, she decided to try earthworms. She had heard of people eating a tonic made of them to cure various maladies. And, besides, she could find them easily.

She went to a large tree near the house and began to dig around its base. In no time at all, she filled a large rice bowl and returned home.

Carefully she washed the worms and put some in the rice pot and made soup with the rest. The smell of the rice cooking reminded her of steaming sweet potatoes. When the rice was cooked, she tasted it and then the soup to make sure they were all right. She then prepared a small dinner table and took it to Mother. Anxiously she watched her eat.

After a few spoonfuls, Mother said, "This is very good. It seems you found something new on the mountain." Daughter-in-law breathed a sigh of relief and returned to the kitchen.

Daughter-in-law continued to gather earthworms for their meals. After a few days, Mother's face took on a healthy glow and her skin became less dry. One day, she surprised Daughter-in-law by saying she would like to go outside because her back didn't hurt any more. Even more astonishing, she walked around the yard several times.

Then one day Son returned home with a large bundle of supplies. He was surprised to hear laughter coming from his house and was even more surprised by his mother's healthy appearance.

"I can't believe how good Mother looks. She even looks like she gained weight. I can't imagine what you fed her, knowing we didn't have any food and there couldn't have been much on the mountains," Son told his wife when they were alone. But she didn't say a word.

Later, Mother told him, "I don't think there is a better daughter-in-law anywhere in this world. Though times were difficult while you were gone, she fed me meat and meat soup everyday. It was delicious and I now feel much better."

"Meat and meat soup?" he asked with amazement.

"Yes. It tasted earthy, like a root. But it was meat. Anyway, I saved some for you. It's in the closet."

Daughter-in-law's face turned bright red as she hung her head. Mother shuffled to the closet and felt around inside it. "Here, try this," she said, thrusting a bowl toward her son. "It's delicious."

Son looked in the bowl and his face went ashen. "Worms! You fed my mother worms!" he exclaimed at his wife who was so distressed she just nodded her head without looking up.

On hearing this, Mother retched several times, and each time the strain pulled her eyes open wide.

"What's happening?" she cried. "Am I dreaming? Is this real? I can see! I can see! I can see my wonderful son! And my wonderful daughter-in-law! I can see!" she exclaimed over and over. The three were so happy they embraced and wept tears of joy.

They all lived comfortably after that and Mother was able to see her grandchildren for *Hanŭnim* restored her eyesight because he was so impressed with Daughter-in-law's filial devotion.

The Faithful Daughter Shim Ch'ŏng

O nce upon a time in a village near the sea there lived a beautiful young girl named Shim Ch'ŏng. She lived with her blind father who was called Shim-*pongsa*, *pongsa* denoting a blind person. Her mother died when she was only a few days old so her father carried her from house to house for mothers to suckle and begged food for himself. Shim Ch'ŏng was thus well-known and liked by all the villagers.

Her charming ways and devotion to her blind father attracted the attention of a nobleman's wife. She gave her odd jobs and finally asked her to work as a maid. So every morning Shim Ch'ŏng went to the nobleman's house and returned home around sundown.

Then one day she didn't come home on time so Shim-*pongsa*, fearing she had had an accident, went out to meet her. Tapping with his walking stick, he found the narrow foot bridge across the stream but, in his haste, stumbled and fell into the water.

"Help! Help! Save me! I'm drowning!" he shouted as he floundered in the water.

A monk passing nearby heard his shouts and came to his rescue. On learning that he was blind, the monk helped him return home. As he was leaving, he muttered to himself, "If only he would offer Buddha three hundred sacks of rice, his sight would be restored."

"What did you say?" exclaimed Shim-*pongsa*.

The monk explained and excitedly Shim-*pongsa* promised Buddha such an offering.

As he waited for Shim Ch'ŏng to return, Shim-*pongsa* worried about his promise to Buddha. "How could I have made such a promise! I don't know what possessed me to do it! I'm just a foolish old man!" he told himself over and over.

Shim Ch'ŏng finally returned, saying she was late because there was a celebration at the nobleman's house. She served her father some delicacies she had brought from the feast but he only picked at them and was unusually quiet.

"What's wrong, Father?" she asked. "Do you feel ill? Or did something happen today?"

"No! Nothing!" he exclaimed.

"I know something is troubling you. Please tell me what it is, Father. Please," she pleaded.

So Shim-*pongsa* explained about the monk and the promise he made to Buddha.

"I don't know how I'll ever be able to make such a large offering. But I must. I must. He promised Buddha. I have to get the rice somehow," Shim Ch'ŏng told herself over and over. And so every day she prayed to all the spirits for help.

Then one day she overheard a woman tell another woman that some sailors were looking for a young virgin to sacrifice to the Dragon King so that they could safely navigate the rough seas to China and that they were willing to pay any price. She quickly asked where she could find the sailors and set off in search of them.

The sailors could not believe that a girl was willingly offering herself to be sacrificed. They listened in awe to her story and were impressed by her devotion to her father and willingness to do anything to have his sight restored.

The sailors agreed to pay her three hundred sacks of rice in exchange for her life and told her they would sail on the next full moon. Happily she watched them load the bags of rice to take them to the temple.

She raced home to tell her father that she had made the promised offering. But her heart skipped a beat when he asked how she obtained the rice.

Although she had never been dishonest, she could not bring herself to tell him the truth. She bit her bottom lip and said, "The nobleman's wife wants to adopt me, so she gave me the rice as payment." Then she quickly added, "I will move to their house on the next full moon."

"That's wonderful," said Shim-*pongsa*, thinking that they would take good care of her and would be very good for her future. "I want you to be happy and not worry about me."

But worry she did. The thought of sacrificing herself to the Dragon King frightened her, but the thought of leaving her father alone broke her heart, for she knew there was no one to take care of him. Every night she sat up until very late mending and washing his clothes and making him new clothes for every season. She replaced the rice paper in the windows and doors and papered over the cracks in the walls and the floors. She washed and mended all the bedding. She did everything she could think of to help her father. And she prayed.

The night before she was to depart she sat beside her father as he slept. Hot tears streamed down her face as she thought of what would become of him. "If only I could prevent the sun from rising, the cock from crowing, the moon from becoming round.... Oh what have I done? What have I done?" she cried over and over to herself.

All too soon she heard a cock crow. And with the first rays of the sun she heard the sailors at her gate.

"I know it is time to go," she told them. "But please allow me to prepare my poor father's breakfast this last time."

The sailors looked at her tear-streaked face and nodded.

With tears burning her eyes, she prepared the best foods she could. "Father, please eat a lot," she said as she placed the food before him.

Shim-*pongsa* ate heartily. After a few spoonfuls he said, "The food tastes especially good. What's the occasion?" But Shim Ch'ŏng remained silent. "I had a dream last night. I saw you riding a carriage pulled by white horses. It must be a good omen. After all, you are moving into the nobleman's house."

"Yes, Father, it must be a good omen," said Shim Ch'ŏng, although she knew full well that it foretold of her coming death. And with that she went to the family altar to bid farewell to her ancestors and ask their forgiveness for abandoning her father. She was so heartbroken she could hardly get to her feet after finishing her bows.

She knelt down beside her father and, overcome with emotion, sobbed loudly.

"What's wrong? There's no need to cry. The nobleman will give you a good home and I'll be fine," he said.

"Oh, Father, forgive me for I have lied," she sobbed. "I'm not going to the nobleman's house. I sold myself to a crew of sailors as a sacrifice to the Dragon King. That's how I got the rice for Buddha's offering."

"No! No! Tell me it's not true!" cried Shim-*pongsa*. "What good is my sight, my life, if I don't have you! You can't go! You can't!"

But it was too late. The sailors were at the door beckoning to Shim Ch'ŏng. She stroked her father's hand and left to the sound of his wailing.

For several days the sea was calm and the sailing smooth. But when they reached an area the sailors called Indangsu, strong waves began to lash the boat with such force it seemed it would break apart. "It's the Dragon King! He's coming to get us!" screamed the sailors and they all stared at Shim Ch'ŏng.

The sailors helped Shim Ch'ŏng climb up onto the bow of the tossing boat. She closed her eyes, clasped her hands in front of her breasts, and jumped. Within seconds, the sea became calm. The sailors stared sadly into the water and then sailed on.

As soon as Shim Ch'ŏng entered the water a sea goddess whisked her off to the Dragon King's palace. The Dragon King gazed admiringly at the unconscious Shim Ch'ŏng and decided to adopt her as his daughter. When she regained consciousness, she was of course frightened but she soon overcame her fear because her surroundings were very beautiful and filled with the sounds of music and laughter. She thanked the Dragon King when he told her he had made her one of his princesses and then told him about her past.

For days she never smiled because her heart was always troubled by thoughts of her father. Finally, the Dragon King could not bear to see her lovely face forever downcast and decided to send her back to the world of men. He had her put in a giant lotus blossom and sent to the surface of the sea.

Some fishermen spotted the flower and hauled it into their boat. After some discussion about its unusual size and how it came to be at sea, they decided to take it to the King.

The King was as amazed as the fishermen. He was even more astonished when the flower suddenly opened and out stepped Shim Ch'ŏng. She too was surprised to find herself before the King.

The King was immediately enamored of her loveliness and determined to marry her. And, indeed, they were soon married.

Shim Ch'ŏng made a beautiful Queen. She was very happy in her new role and loved her King very much. However, she could not help thinking about her poor father and wondering what had become of him.

One day the King was surprised to see tears streaming down her face. At first she wouldn't tell him why she was crying but he was so persistent that she finally told him her entire story.

The King was speechless. Shim Ch'ŏng did not know how to interpret the serious expression that came over his face.

After a while he said, "We'll have a feast for blind people. I'll send out a proclamation for all blind people to attend a feast at the palace. If your father is still living, he will surely come."

Countless blind men came to the palace. They were served delicious foods and entertained by the court musicians. Every day Shim Ch'ŏng looked at the men who came to the feast and every day she was disappointed.

On the last day of the feast, she watched the blind men through teary eyes. Then a tall, thin, shabbily dressed man caught her eye as he stumbled through the gate. She rubbed her eyes and looked again.

To everyone's surprise, she raced through the crowd and threw her arms around him.

"Father! Father!" she cried. "It's me. Shim Ch'ŏng."

"My Daughter? My Ch'ŏng? Is it really you? Let me see!" he cried. And at that very moment his eyes opened wide in amazement and he could see. "I can see!" he shouted. "I can see!"

Everyone wept tears of joy and the King ordered the feast to continue for many days to celebrate the reunion of his Queen and her father.

The Magic Vase

L ong, long ago there was a kind fisherman who was married to a cruel, greedy woman.

One winter day he looked out to sea through the falling snow and shook his head. "This certainly isn't a good day for fishing," he muttered to himself. "I guess I will just mend some nets."

"What are you doing?" asked his wife, stepping out onto the covered porch where he was working. "You better get a move on if you expect to catch any fish," she said sternly.

"Well, you see, since the weather isn't very good, I thought I would stay at home and mend a few nets and do some other things around the house. There really isn't much chance of catching any fish on a foul day like this."

"Pshaw! That's a sorry excuse for wanting to loaf!" shouted his wife. "Now get out of here and bring back some fish!"

"All right. All right," said the fisherman, and he began gathering up his fishing gear.

At sea, the fisherman struggled to throw his net into the water and pull it out. He was frightened because the waves crashed into his boat with such fury that it seemed like the sea would swallow it. Again and again he threw his net into the water to only pull it up empty. Finally he felt something in it but was disappointed to pull in an old vase. He started to throw the vase back into the water but then he stored it carefully in the bow of the boat. He threw his net into the water several more times and then decided to go home.

The fisherman left his boat on the beach and walked home carrying the vase under his arm.

"Why are you carrying that dirty old vase?" cried his wife as soon as she saw him.

"It's all I caught," replied the fisherman. "I told you it was useless to go out today. I didn't pull in a single fish, not even a small one."

"Well, why did you bring that dirty old vase? You should have just thrown it back to the sea."

"I thought we could clean it up and use it. It's really not bad looking," said the fisherman as he stepped up onto the porch and swung open the door.

"Just where do you think you're going to put that ugly thing?" stormed the woman, following him inside. "I don't want it in here," she shouted and tried to grab the vase.

"Oh, come on now," said the fisherman. "Just let me..."

P'ŏng! came a loud noise from the vase and the room filled with smoke.

"What's happening?" cried the fisherman as the vase jumped out of his hands.

"Who, who, who's that?" whispered the woman.

"Don't be frightened," said a young man standing before them. "I'm your helper. If you have any wish, just rub the vase three times and say what it is. I can grant you three wishes."

P'ŏng! The young man and the smoke disappeared into the vase.

"How wonderful! How wonderful!" shouted the woman, jumping up and down. "Rice! Rice! Let's ask for rice!"

"Yes. Yes. Let's ask for rice," said the fisherman and he rubbed the vase three times and asked for rice. At once a mountain of rice filled the yard.

The fisherman and his wife danced happily until they slumped down on the rice, out of breath. After a while the woman grabbed the vase and rubbed it.

P'ŏng! The young man appeared in a cloud of smoke.

Smiling broadly the woman said, "Make us the richest people in this village."

"Look inside your house," said the young man and he disappeared as before.

The woman rushed into the house. "Wow!" she screamed. Gold and silver coins and all kinds of jewelry and precious gems covered the floor. "What a wonderful vase!" she cried as she sat down and began tossing coins and jewels into the air. "It's wonderful! Just wonderful!"

After a while she turned to her husband and said, "Go see if you can catch another vase like this one."

"What?" cried the fisherman. "Have you gone mad? You've got all this wealth and you want more. You shouldn't be so greedy."

"We can only use the vase one more time and there are still lots of things I want. If you don't catch one, don't even think of coming home!" snorted the woman.

The fisherman grabbed up his gear and left, shaking his head and frowning.

The woman sat in front of a mirror, draping jewelry around her neck and admiring her riches. Suddenly she threw the mirror on the floor and shrieked, "Why am I so ugly?" After a while she slapped her knee and grabbed the vase. "I should have thought of that before?" she cried, and quickly rubbed the vase three times.

P'ŏng! The young man appeared. "Now what can I do for you?" he grinned.

"Make me beautiful," said the woman.

Without a word, the young man nodded his head and disappeared into the vase.

The woman grabbed up her mirror and looked at herself. She laughed and laughed. "I'm as pretty as a young girl," she giggled, turning from side to side to look at herself in the mirror. Suddenly she frowned. "Now that I'm so pretty, how can I live with that ugly husband of mine? If he comes back with another vase, I'll just have to get rid of him."

Chuckling to herself, she looked at her mirror again. "Oh no! My face!" she shrieked at the reflection of her old self.

A strong wind began to blow and blew away all the jewels and coins, the rice, the house, the woman and everything.

At sea, the fisherman sat in his tossing boat, thinking about his greedy wife. Something dark caught his eye. It was a large turtle.

The turtle swam around and around the little boat. It seemed to be motioning for the fisherman to get on its back. The fisherman watched it for a while and then got on its back. It dove at once and carried the fisherman to the Dragon King's palace at the bottom of the sea.

The Dragon King invited the fisherman to live in his palace and gave him a loving wife. He lived a long and happy life.

The Grateful Magpies

I n a certain village deep in the mountains there lived a kind and studious young man. Although they were very poor, his parents encouraged him to study hard in the hope that he would pass the *kwagŏ.**

Finally, after many years of diligent study, the young man departed on foot for Hanyang, the nation's capital, to take the examination. He carried a bow and arrows in case he was attacked by a wild animal along the way.

One day as he was walking along, he noticed a pair of magpies darting up and down at a limb of a pine tree and cawing as if something were wrong. He moved closer to get a better look and saw a large snake slithering toward a nest containing several baby magpies. He quickly set his bow and shot an arrow into the snake's head. He retrieved his arrow and continued on his way for he knew that it would soon be dark and he needed to find a place to stay the night.

As the sun went down he quickened his steps because he didn't want to spend the night outside. "I've got to find shelter," he told himself over and over, glancing here and there in the hope of spotting a light.

Finally, when he was just about to give up finding a place,

---

* *Kwagŏ:* the national government examination by which a man qualified for appointment to a position in the bureaucracy.

he saw the faint glow of a light in the distance. He was disappointed to find that it was not a house but an old dilapidated temple building. It gave him an eerie feeling. Nevertheless, he called out, "Is anyone here? I'm a wayfarer in need of a place to sleep."

The door opened and a tall, thin woman in white stepped out. "I can't provide any food, but you're welcome to stay the night."

"Thank you. I just need a place to lay my head," said the young man, thinking he was lucky to have found shelter and wondering what a young woman was doing alone there. The woman showed him to a room and left.

He was asleep as soon as he lay down. After a while his breathing became labored and he began to wake up. He felt like something heavy was pressing on his chest. He opened his eyes to a horrifying sight.

A large snake was coiled up on his chest. Its red eyes stared at him as its forked tongue darted in and out. "You killed my husband! Now I am going to kill you!" it hissed and began coiling itself around the young man's throat.

"Oh, please! Please don't kill me!" pleaded the young man.

"Why should I spare you?" snarled the snake. "You killed my husband!"

"I know how you feel," said the young man, trying to reason with the snake. "I know you want to revenge your husband's death. But please don't kill me. I'm on my way to Hanyang to take the *kwagŏ*. You see my parents have struggled for a long time so that I could study for it. Just think how bereaved they would be if I died before taking it. Please have pity on me."

"Pity?" hissed the snake. "Why should I have pity on you? You killed my husband and now you must pay for it with your life!" snarled the snake and began squeezing the young man's neck.

"No! No!" begged the young man. "I killed him because he was going to eat the baby magpies. They looked so pitiful I couldn't let him eat them. You must understand. They were just tiny babies and I felt pity for them. That's the only reason I did it."

The snake stared at the young man for a while and then loosened its hold slightly. "I can see that you like animals. But I cannot forget that you killed my husband. That is unforgivable. But I will give you a chance. There's a bell tower on the hill behind here. If you can make the bell ring three times before midnight, you can live," hissed the snake and slithered off into the darkness.

The young man frantically rushed outside. But it was difficult for him to find his way up the hill in the pitch dark. He finally reached the top but was disheartened to discover that the steps of the dilapidated bell tower had crumbled. He sighed deeply. "I've got to get up there. I..."

"Well, well, only a few more seconds," hissed the snake which, undetected by the young man, had curled up near his ankle ready to strike. Its forked tongue darted in and out between its fangs and its eyes glowed in the dark.

Ttaeng! Ttaeng! Ttaeng! Rang the bell.

The snake stared at the young man. "I truly want to kill you! But I will keep my promise," it hissed and disappeared into the darkness.

At dawn the young man returned to the bell tower. Thinking Buddha had saved him, he knelt down on the ground to express his thanks. He was surprised to see two dead magpies. They were covered with dew and their necks and heads were broken. Tears streaked down the young man's cheeks for he now understood who was responsible for ringing the bell.

The Queen Swallow's Gift

Hŭng-bu and Nol-bu were brothers. They and their families lived together with their elderly father, a wealthy landowner. Nol-bu was the oldest.

One day the brothers were called to their father's bedside. "My sons," he said in a raspy voice, "it is time for me to leave this world. I want the two of you and your families to live in harmony together, sharing everything equally. That is all I ask." After a few moments of labored breathing, he closed his eyes and died.

Hŭng-bu and Nol-bu buried him on a mountain slope behind their house. It was an auspicious spot overlooking a stream. As soon as they returned home from the burial ceremony, Nol-bu searched his father's room and took everything of value he could find.

From that day on, Nol-bu and his wife treated Hŭng-bu and his family like servants. Hŭng-bu's wife had to do all the cooking, cleaning and washing and his children had to do all the chores and run all the errands. Nol-bu's family ate first and Hŭng-bu's family had to make do with the leftovers. If Hŭng-bu's children cried for more food, Nol-bu's wife would slap them and say they had eaten more than their share.

Then one day Nol-bu's wife said to him, "Those brats of Hŭng-bu's are going to be the ruin of us."

"What's that? The ruin of us?" asked Nol-bu.

"Those kids of Hŭng-bu's. They eat so much there is never anything left. They're going to be the ruin of us."

"Then I guess I'll just have to do something about them," replied Nol-bu, frowning and stroking his chin. "Hŭng-bu!" he screamed after a few minutes. "Come here! I want to see you at once!"

Hŭng-bu hurried to the open hall where Nol-bu was sitting but before he could get his shoes off to enter Nol-bu jumped up and began yelling. "I want you and your family out of this house," he shouted, shaking his pipe at Hŭng-bu. "You and your brats have been a burden long enough. Now get out! Be gone with you!" With those words, he turned quickly and walked into his study.

A shocked Hŭng-bu helped his wife and crying children gather up what few belongings they had. They left the house to the sound of the resounding bang of the gate as Nol-bu's grinning wife slammed it behind them.

They wandered from one place to another until they stumbled upon a rundown old shack which was hardly large enough for them all to lie down. They made a game of trying to find things with which to mend the roof and in no time it was repaired.

Hŭng-bu did odd jobs at houses in nearby villages and his wife and children gathered wild vegetables, mushrooms and berries for their meals. However, Hŭng-bu and his wife began to worry as the autumn nights got colder and it became more and more difficult to find food.

Finally Hŭng-bu's wife said, "Please go to your brother's house and get something, even if it is only barley."

Hŭng-bu hated the thought of facing his brother but he hated facing his starving children even more so the next morning he went to Nol-bu's house.

"Please, Brother, spare us a few bags of barley," he said, looking up at Nol-bu who was standing on the porch. "We don't have anything to eat. Please give me something."

"I'll give you something," Nol-bu said haughtily, stepping down from the porch. "Take this, you no-good-for-nothing bum! Take this!" he yelled, hitting Hŭng-bu over and over with a stick. "Get out, you bum! Get out! And don't come begging around here again!"

Leaving the house, Hŭng-bu passed by the kitchen. At that very moment Nol-bu's wife was putting hot steamy rice into a bowl.

"Oh, Sister-in-law," called Hŭng-bu, sticking his head inside the doorway, "please give me a scoop of rice."

In a flash, Nol-bu's wife hit Hŭng-bu's cheek with the rice scoop. "Get out of here, you bum! Get out!" she shrieked.

"Oh, thank you, Sister-in-law. Thank you for hitting me with the rice scoop." Hŭng-bu laughed as he pulled some rice from his cheek and stuck it in his mouth. "Won't you hit this cheek, too," he said, laughing and turning his other cheek to her.

Quickly wiping the scoop on her apron, she swung at Hŭng-bu's other cheek but hit the doorframe because he ducked. Hŭng-bu laughed as he ran through the yard and out the gate, pulling the remaining grains of rice from his face and eating them.

Somehow Hŭng-bu and his family made it through the long cold winter. They were happy when spring finally arrived because they could gather roots and plants to eat. To their delight, a pair of swallows made a nest in the eaves of their roof. In a few weeks the nest was home to several baby swallows who chirped constantly for food.

One day when Hŭng-bu returned home from working in a nearby field, he noticed a big snake near the corner of the house. He killed it with a hoe. Then he realized that he didn't hear any chirping coming from under the eaves.

He looked into the nest. It was empty. Then he looked on the ground. There was one of the tiny swallows. Hŭng-bu knew at once what had happened. The snake had eaten the other babies but in doing so had pushed this one out of the nest.

Hŭng-bu picked up the baby swallow and examined it. One of its legs was broken. Hŭng-bu gently bound the leg with string and put the bird back in its nest. The children lovingly cared for it, feeding it worms and insects, and soon it was flittering around the yard. In late autumn it flew southward with all the other birds.

The next spring Hŭng-bu and his family were glad to see the birds return for it meant the end of another long, hard winter. One warm day a lone swallow perched on their roof and chirped loudly. Then it flew in a circle around their yard several times, dropped a seed at Hŭng-bu's feet and flew away. Hŭng-bu and his family carefully planted the seed and looked forward to eating gourds come autumn.

The seed, a gift from the Queen Swallow to repay Hŭng-bu's kindness, grew quickly into a vine and soon there were three small gourds on it. Hŭng-bu and his wife were surprised at how fast and big the gourds grew. By autumn, when the gourds were ripe enough to eat, they were so big that Hŭng-bu and his children had to use a saw to cut them.

Happily they cut the first gourd. They couldn't believe their eyes. Out tumbled strings of gold and silver coins, all kinds of precious jewels, and silk and brocade fabrics. Once they were over their surprise, they cut the second gourd. At once the yard became filled with sacks of rice. They cut the last gourd. Out marched hundreds of tiny carpenters. Within a few minutes they constructed a large tile-roofed house surrounded by a wall with a large gate and then disappeared. Hŭng-bu and his family danced for joy. They were wealthy!

Word of Hŭng-bu's newfound wealth spread quickly throughout the nearby villages and soon reached Nol-bu. It made him very cross and finally he could not stand it any longer—he had to go see for himself.

Nol-bu stood in wonder in front of the impressive tile-roofed gate. Shaking his head, he walked up to it and called loudly, "Hŭng-bu! Hŭng-bu! Let me in!"

Hŭng-bu welcomed Nol-bu as if nothing had ever happened and while they talked in Hŭng-bu's study, his wife served them persimmon tea. Finally Nol-bu could not restrain himself and he blurted out, "How could a bum like you become wealthy overnight? Come on, tell me the truth. Who did you rob?"

Hŭng-bu told him about the swallow dropping the seed and how they planted it and were so surprised when they cut open the gourds. "All I can imagine is that the swallow must have been the one whose leg I bandaged."

"What's that?" asked Nol-bu. "You say you bandaged a swallow's leg and it gave you the magic seed?"

"Well, I'm not exactly sure," said Hŭng-bu and then he explained about the swallow falling out of the nest.

"Let me get this straight," said Nol-bu. "A pair of swallows built a nest under the eaves of your roof. When the birds hatched, a snake crawled into the nest and ate all of the birds but one which fell onto the ground and broke its leg. Then you bandaged the leg and when it healed the bird flew away and the next spring brought you a magic gourd seed."

"It seems that way," smiled Hŭng-bu.

"I see," said Nol-bu, stroking his chin pensively. After a few moments silence, he jumped up and said he had to leave.

From that day on, Nol-bu's thoughts were filled with images of swallows and magic gourd seeds. Spring finally ar-

rived and he and his wife waited anxiously for a pair of swallows to build a nest under the eaves of their house. They even scattered a variety of grains in the yard and on the rooftop in the hope of attracting a pair. At long last a pair of swallows did build a nest under their eaves and in a few weeks it was home to several baby birds.

Every day Nol-bu watched for a snake to raid the nest and every day he was disappointed. Then one day he decided he had waited long enough for a snake to come. He took one of the babies from the nest and broke one of its legs with his bare hands. Then he bound up the leg with some cord and, saying, "Okay, you little bird, I fixed your broken leg so next spring bring me a magic gourd seed," placed it back in its nest. The bird recovered and flew southward in the autumn.

Spring arrived and Nol-bu watched for the swallow to return. Finally a lone swallow came. It flew around the yard and then dropped a seed at Nol-bu's feet and flew away. Nol-bu was ecstatic. He shouted to his wife to come out and together they planted the seed. All summer they watched the seed grow into a vine and three of the biggest gourds they had ever seen ripen on it.

Autumn arrived and it was finally time to open the gourds. Talking about how wealthy they were going to be, they sawed open the first gourd. Out jumped hundreds of beggars. In the blink of an eye they were all over the house, eating every edible thing they could find.

"This can't be!" screamed Nol-bu. "Something is wrong. There's been a mistake."

"Surely there must be gold in the next gourd," cried his wife.

Quickly they sawed open the next gourd. Out poured putrid night soil and covered them from head to foot. But still they did not give up. Slipping and sliding in the foul smelling muck, they sawed open the last gourd. Out tumbled an army of ogres carrying large spiny mallets and at once they began breaking down Nol-bu's house. When nothing was left standing, they hit Nol-bu and his wife until they passed out. Then they disappeared along with the beggars.

Ironically, on that very day, Hŭng-bu and his wife decided to pay a visit to Nol-bu to try to make bygones be bygones. They were shocked to find the house in a shambles. They searched through the rubble and found Nol-bu and his wife.

They gently propped them up and gave them some water. After a few moments they regained consciousness. Nol-bu looked into Hŭng-bu's eyes and said, "I was wrong, Hŭng-bu. I was wrong. Please forgive me."

"Don't talk now," said Hŭng-bu. "Just rest. You and your family can come live with us. Everything will be fine."

From that day on, Hŭng-bu and Nol-bu became the best of brothers and their families lived happily together.

An Ox for a Persimmon

I n a certain place there lived two men by the name of Kim and Pak. Mr. Kim was kind and caring and Mr. Pak was greedy and cunning.

Beside Mr. Kim's house was the stump of a persimmon tree. He watered it every morning and evening and fertilized it with manure. It grew rapidly into a strong, healthy tree and, to everyone's surprise, tiny persimmons appeared on its branches.

In the autumn, villagers came daily to gaze in wonder at the watermelon-size persimmons ripening on the tree. When they were finally ripe enough to harvest, Mr. Kim picked each one with great care and filled many large sacks.

The sight of the bulging sacks filled his heart with joy and he happily shared the persimmons with his neighbors. Then, thinking the persimmons were truly unusual, he carefully wrapped up the largest one and set out for Hanyang to deliver it to the King.

The King stared in disbelief when the Royal Secretary placed the persimmon before him. "I've never seen such a large persimmon. It's magnificent. The man who grew it deserves an award. Is there anything as big as this among the gifts I've received lately?"

"Yes, Your Majesty, there is. But, Your Majesty, it is quite rare and very valuable," said the Royal Secretary.

"Well, aren't you going to tell me what it is?" exclaimed

the King.

"Yes, of course, Your Majesty. It's just...that...well...it is a gold nugget."

"Well, that's no problem. Present it to the man at once."

So it was that Mr. Kim returned home with a gold nugget as big as a watermelon. News of his good fortune spread quickly through the village.

The greedy Mr. Pak was overcome with jealousy and made up his mind to take the King something so that he too would be awarded a gold nugget. He pondered what would be good to take. Finally, he sold all his property in order to purchase it and set out for Hanyang with visions of a gold nugget as big as an ox swirling in his head.

"This ox looks like a fine animal. And it's very large," said the King when the Royal Secretary presented Mr. Pak's gift to him. "I shall give the man who brought it an award. What have I received recently that I can give him?"

"Well, Your Majesty, there is that watermelon-size persimmon you received a few days ago," replied the Royal Secretary.

"Oh, yes. That will do nicely," said the King.

Mr. Pak fainted when the Royal Secretary presented him with the persimmon. And that is how he became a poor man.

A Monk Gets a Surprise

There was once a lovely young woman who lived with her widowed mother along the route to a provincial capital. She had one dream—to marry a governor. But being of low birth, there was very little chance of that happening. Whenever she told her mother of her aspiration, her mother would laugh and say, "Stop dreaming of rice cakes."

Nonetheless, the woman did not give up her dream. She even began going to a nearby temple to pray to Buddha to help her marry a governor.

One day a wicked monk saw her enter the main hall of the temple. Attracted by her beauty, he sneaked into the hall and hid behind the main image of Buddha to watch her.

"*Namuamit'abul,** please help me marry a governor," she prayed aloud over and over.

Presently, the monk said in a deep voice, "Do as I say and you will have your wish. A monk will come to your house three days from now. You must do as he instructs. You must go with him."

The young woman was frightened to hear the statue speak but she was also excited. She rushed home, repeating what

---

* *Namuamit'abul:* a Buddhist chant that has several meanings depending on the circumstances: here it means, "I believe in Amitabha (the Buddha of Infinite Light)."

she had heard over and over to herself, and did not notice the monk following close behind her.

She bubbled with joy as she told her mother that Buddha had spoken to her. "I don't like the idea of you going off with a monk whom we know nothing about," said her mother. "But Buddha would never lead you astray."

Three days later a monk appeared at their gate. He carried a large wooden box on his back. "Buddha sent me," he told the mother. "I am to take your daughter to my temple. She must get inside this box so I can carry her."

The mother and daughter looked at each other with tear-filled eyes and embraced. Then the mother said, "We should not question what Buddha has ordained. Get into the box."

The young woman got into the box without a word. The monk put the lid on, tied it with a rope to make shoulder straps and hoisted it onto his back. He smiled at the mother and left.

Happily he walked down the road, visions of the woman's loveliness filling his head. Then he spotted a large, official looking procession headed his way. He lowered the box to the side of the road and ran off into the forest.

Unknown to the monk, it was a hunting party led by none other than the Governor of the province. They were returning from a hunting expedition with two dead tigers and a live one.

The Governor had noticed the monk's strange behavior so he stopped his horse when he came to the box and dismounted. He ordered the box opened and watched curiously as the men untied the rope and lifted the lid. The men jumped back in surprise as the young woman stood up and looked around.

"My dear girl," said the Governor, "what are you doing in that box?"

"Oh, but don't you know? I was on my way to marry

you, Your Excellency," she replied in a demure voice. "You *are* the Governor, *aren't* you?"

"Well, yes, of course," said the Governor flabbergasted. "But what do you mean you were on the way to marry me?"

"I prayed to Buddha..." the girl explained the story to the Governor.

With a twinkle in his eye, the Governor told his men to put the live tiger in the box and tie the lid on in the fashion they had found it. Then they all journeyed on to the provincial capital with the woman riding in a palanquin.

After a while the monk returned and picked up his box. Happily he carried it to a small hermitage near his temple.

"Oh, my lovely, I have waited so long for this moment. At long last I have a woman," exclaimed the monk as he fumbled with the rope. At last he got the rope untied and lifted the lid. The tiger sprang out and bit his throat all in one swift movement.

Meanwhile, the Governor and the woman arrived at his office. They talked for a while and then the Governor said, "You may not be of noble birth, but apparently we were destined to marry. You see, I, too, prayed to Buddha. I prayed to him because my wife recently died during childbirth and I wanted to remarry. I prayed to him to send me a nice, healthy young woman and here you are. You prayed for a governor, and here I am. It must be Buddha's will that we marry."

And so it was that the young woman of lowly birth married the Governor. They had many children and lived a long, prosperous life.

The Man Who Became an Ox

L ong ago in a farming village at the foot of a mountain there lived a man who hated work. The shiftless fellow loved nothing better than lazing around the house all day. Even during the planting and harvesting, when his wife and children and all the other villagers were working hard in the fields from dawn to dusk, Lazybones, as he was often called, would spend the day sleeping or lying in the shade of a big tree, playing with twigs and sprigs of grass.

One day his wife, who was sick of his idleness and of the jokes the neighbors made about him, said in a stern voice, "Stop loafing and go work in the fields. Everyone else is working hard to get the fields plowed and the crops planted. You should work too."

Lazybones frowned and rolled over so his back was to his wife.

"I doubt that there is another person as lazy as you in the world. When living is even difficult for those who work hard, how can we live if all you do is loaf? How can we survive?"

"Hush woman. Don't bother me. Can't you see I'm trying to rest?"

"Bother you? I'm only trying to get you to do what a man is born to do. How can a person live if he hates work?" After a few moments she left to go plant rice with her neighbors.

Lazybones decided he could not stand his wife's nagging and thought about running far away. Suddenly he jumped up and rushed over to a chest in the corner of the room and took two rolls of hemp cloth from it. Smiling broadly, he walked out of the house, carrying the cloth which his wife had stayed up many nights to make. "I can sell this cloth to get enough to live on for a long time," he happily told himself.

Lazybones set off on a path leading across the mountain behind his house. Shortly after crossing the first pass, he came to a small thatched house that had not been there before. The closer he got to it, the more curious he became for he could see in the yard an old man making a very strange looking thing.

"What's that you're making?" called Lazybones.

The old man looked up and grinned. "Why? Do you find it interesting?"

"No, it's just that that thing is so queer looking," said Lazybones, moving closer to the old man. "What is it?"

"Well, if you really want to know, I'll tell you," said the old man. "It's an ox head mask."

"An ox head mask?" laughed Lazybones. "Why on earth are you making such a useless thing?"

The old man chuckled. "Listen, if it were useless, I wouldn't have made it."

"Silly old man. You should just relax instead of making such a useless thing," said Lazybones and he started to walk away, laughing.

"If anyone who hates work puts on this mask, something really good will happen to him," said the old man nonchalantly.

Lazybones stopped in his tracks. "Did you say that if someone who hates work puts on that mask, something good

will happen to him?"

"That's what I said," replied the old man and he smiled and stroked the mask.

"You really mean it?" asked Lazybones as he moved closer to the old man. "It's true?"

"Here, try it on," said the old man, holding the mask out toward Lazybones. "After all, it's better to try something once than to hear about it a hundred times."

With the words "something good will happen" echoing in his ears, Lazybones grabbed the mask and quickly pulled it on over his head. In the blink of an eye, the old man threw the ox hide on which he had been sitting on Lazybones back.

Immediately Lazybones began to feel strange. He tried to pull the mask off but it wouldn't come off. Then he felt the ox hide squeezing his shoulders and hips. "What's happening? What's happening? Take this thing off! Help me! Help me! I must be sick!" he screamed. He wriggled and shook but the hide would not come off, it just kept stretching and tightening until it covered him completely.

The old man stood up and brushed off his clothes. Then he picked up a rope and tied it around Lazybones' neck.

"Let me go," cried Lazybones. "Let me go!" But the only sound that came from his mouth was a loud "Moo."

"Okay, fellow. Come on now. Let's go," said the old man, pulling the rope around Lazybones' neck.

"No! No! Let me go!" yelled Lazybones but all he could hear coming from his mouth was the bellowing of an ox. He tried to run away but he wasn't used to running on all fours.

The old man hit Lazybones' rump with a stick. "Stop that! You're an ox now and you should behave like one. Do what I say and I won't hit you. Now come on." The old man pulled hard on the rope around Lazybones' neck and led him down the nearest path.

They walked a long way through the forest. Every once in a while Lazybones tried to run away but the old man held the rope tight and hit him with a stick.

Finally they came to a small town. It was market day so the place was teeming with farmers and traders. The old man led Lazybones to a lot where there were many cows and oxen and tied him to a stake. Lazybones looked around and wondered what they were doing there. Then he realized that the old man was going to sell him.

Soon there were many men admiring him for he had become a fine looking ox. Each and every one prodded him with a stick and looked at his feet and his teeth.

After some bargaining, the old man untied Lazybones' rope from the stake and handed it to a farmer. "He's a little headstrong but he'll make a good worker," said the old man and he slapped Lazybones on the rump. "And, by the way, don't give him any turnips."

"Why's that?" asked the farmer.

"If he eats turnip, he'll die right on the spot," said the old man.

"He'll die if he eats turnip. I've never heard of such an ox," said the farmer. But he could not back out of the deal since he had already paid the old man. Shaking his head, he led Lazybones away.

The next morning the farmer led Lazybones from the stall where he had spent the night to a field and hooked a plow to him. All day Lazybones had to pull the heavy plow back and forth across the field. Every time he tried to rest, the farmer hit him with a stick. And, when he tried to tell the farmer he wasn't an ox, the farmer just hit him harder because, of course, the only sound that came out of his mouth was a loud bellow. At sundown the farmer led him back to his stall and gave him some fodder. He was so tired and hungry and sad that he slumped down on the ground and cried himself to sleep.

Every day, shortly after the first cock-crow, the farmer drove him off to the fields for a day of grueling, backbreaking work. At sundown it was back to his stall for a meal of smelly fodder.

After several days, Lazybones was unable to sleep at night. He would lie awake thinking about his family and his situation. Then one night he told himself, "This is all my fault. I turned into an ox because I was so lazy. All I ever wanted was to loaf. Now I have to do someone else's work. It's all because I was so lazy and worthless." He decided he would rather die than go on living under such difficult conditions. But that was not easy to do either.

Then one day as he was walking to a new field, he noticed a turnip patch beside the path. At once he recalled the words of the old man: "If he eats turnip, he'll die right on the spot." As he pulled the plow up and down the field all day, the old man's words kept ringing in his ears.

When he and the farmer came near the turnip patch on their way home, he suddenly jerked as hard as he could and pulled the rope out of the farmer's hand. He rushed to the turnip patch and gobbled down two turnips before the farmer could come to his senses.

At once Lazybones began to feel strange. He shook his head and the mask fell off. He shook his body and the ox hide fell off. He stood upright and looked down at his body. "I'm a man again! I'm a man again," he shouted happily and jumped up and down in front of the startled farmer.

Lazybones told the farmer about the old man and the ox head mask and then they parted.

On his way home, Lazybones looked for the cottage where he had met the old man but there was no trace of it. However, he did find the two rolls of hemp cloth he had taken from his home lying on a rock where he had left them.

When he got home, his wife was overjoyed to see him. She asked over and over where he had been, but he was too embarrassed to tell her and moreover he didn't think she would believe him if he did tell her. From that day on he worked harder than anyone in the village and he and his wife lived a long and happy life.

The Fountain of Youth

In the long-ago days in a hamlet deep in the mountains there lived an uncommonly kind elderly couple. They had no children so, despite their advanced age, they had to support themselves. They sold wood to make a living, there being little arable land in the area. They never complained about their hard lot and were always willing to help others. The villagers had only good to say about them and thought that it was unfortunate Heaven had not blessed them with children.

A greedy, cantankerous old widower lived beside the couple. Like them, he was also childless. However, because of his ill-temper and selfish ways, he was not well liked by the villagers, except the old couple.

One day when the kind old man was cutting wood in the forest, he was suddenly attracted by the sound of a bird singing. He had never heard a more beautiful bird's song. Pulling out his pipe, he sat down to rest and listen to the bird sing.

After a while, the bird flew away, much to the old man's disappointment. But in no time at all he could hear faintly the crystalline notes of its song. Wanting to listen more, he got up and walked in the direction from which the sound came. But when he reached the tree where the bird was perched, it flew away. The old man followed. Again and again the bird flew from tree to tree, and again and again the old man followed, deeper and deeper into the forest. Finally, the bird did not fly away. It perched in a tree beside a bubbling spring and sang even more beautifully than before.

The old man sat down under the tree to listen. After a short time he felt very thirsty. He knelt down beside the spring and, cupping some water in his hand, drank. The water was very sweet and cold so he drank several times.

At once he began to feel the same way he did whenever he drank good rice wine. At the same time he began to feel drowsy so he lay down on a large flat rock near the spring to rest a few minutes and at once he fell into a sound sleep.

When at last he awoke, the sun had already set and darkness was spreading quickly throughout the forest. He looked around and wondered where he was. Then he remembered following the bird and drinking the spring water.

He hurried off in the direction from which he thought he had come and soon reached the place where he had been cutting trees. His legs felt unusually strong and his body felt lighter. He crouched under his A-frame carrier which was loaded with wood, put his arms through its straps and stood up with it on his back. He was surprised at how light it was and, with a spring in his steps, set off down the path for home.

Meanwhile, at home, his wife had begun to worry because it was long past the time for him to return. Pacing back and forth, she imagined all kinds of tragedies had befallen him. Finally, she went next door.

"Old Man," she said, "my husband isn't back yet. Do you think he could have hurt himself? Or maybe a tiger got him?"

Instead of saying something to ease her mind, the old man said flatly, "Humph, it is late. Surely a tiger or a wolf got him."

The old woman asked the old man to go with her to look for her husband but he refused. She returned home and prepared to go into the forest alone to look. Just as she was putting on a shawl to go out she heard someone whistling. She rushed to the gate and saw her husband coming down the trail. With a long sigh of relief, she went out to meet him.

Once inside the house, the old woman looked at her husband in disbelief. "Wha, wha, wha," she stuttered but she couldn't say anything more.

"Hey, what's going on? What's the matter with you?" asked the old man.

"No, it can't be. Is it you, Old Man? Is it really you?"

"Of course it's me! What kind of crazy talk is this? Have you gone mad?"

"You're so young! Your face doesn't have a single wrinkle!"

The old man put his hands to his face and touched his cheeks and rubbed his forehead. It was true. He didn't have any wrinkles. His skin felt soft and sleek like a young person's. "Ah, so that's why my A-frame felt so light coming home."

"What's going on, Old Man? Did something happen while you were in the forest?"

The old man told her all about the bird and drinking the spring water and waking up to find himself by the spring.

"That must be it, Old Man. That strange water made you young." The old woman smiled and nodded her head over and over. But then she frowned. "What about me? Look at me. Don't you think I should drink some of that spring water, too? Otherwise the villagers will make fun of us, a young man living with this old woman."

The two set off immediately to find the spring. The old man helped his wife kneel down beside the pool of water and, with his cupped hands, gave her several drinks. At once she turned into a young woman. They were overjoyed to be young again and vowed right then and there to work harder than they had ever worked before.

Of course their greedy old neighbor was shocked when he saw them and very jealous, too. However, the kind old man explained what had happened and told him the exact location of the spring. Saying, "I, too, must become young and live a long, long time," the greedy old man set off for the spring.

It became late afternoon and the man hadn't returned. So the couple decided to go look for him. They were surprised to hear the sound of a baby crying coming from the direction of the spring. They ran to the spring and were shocked at what they found. There on a large flat rock was a baby dressed in the clothes of their neighbor.

"Oh my, it's the ornery old guy!" said the old man.

"What do you mean it's the ornery old guy?" asked the old woman. "What are you talking about?"

"Well, can't you see for yourself? Apparently the old guy was so greedy he drank too much of the water," said the old man and he began to laugh.

"Oh, of course. That must be it," said the old woman. "He was so anxious to be young that he drank so much water he became a baby."

"It's for sure. Look at the spring," said the old man, pointing to the pool which was almost empty, and he broke into loud guffaws.

His wife laughed too and then she said, "What about the baby, Old Man? Let's raise him as our own."

"That's a wonderful idea," said the old man, picking up the baby. "Let's go home."

The couple worked harder than ever and the baby grew up to be kind and caring.

The Greedy Princess

In times gone by there lived an elderly widow with three sons. They were not wealthy but they lived comfortably.

One day the widow called her sons together and said, "My sons, I don't think I am long for this world. But please don't be sad. I have lived a long and happy life...."

"Mother, are you sick? We can get some medicine," interrupted one of the sons.

"No, no. I'm not sick. I'm just old. So I thought it best to show you something before this old head becomes too fuddled to explain," she said as she reached into a chest beside her and took out a small bundle. "You have never seen these before," she said carefully unwrapping it. "These are treasures that have been in this family for many generations. They are very valuable so you must be very careful. Do not tell anyone about them or show them to anyone."

She placed a large marble on the floor. Then a bamboo flute. And finally a vest which looked the worst for wear. She looked at each one proudly. But the brothers looked at each other in disbelief.

"Mother, those aren't treasures," said the oldest.

"They look like junk," said the second.

Mother smiled knowingly. "I know they don't look like much. But believe me. They have special powers and have served this family well for a long time." She picked up the marble. "Here, I'll show you," she said and rolled the marble across the floor. It left a trail of coins on the floor.

"That's fantastic," cried the oldest.

"We can be rich," cried the second.

"What do the flute and vest do?" cried the third.

"Just a minute! Just a minute!" laughed the widow. "This one is for you," she said, handing the marble to the oldest. "But it must be used sparingly in times of need to help all of you. It is not to be used to make any of you rich. You must understand that."

"I understand," said the oldest, rubbing the marble over and over.

"This flute is for you," said the widow, handing it to the second oldest. "A band of soldiers will appear when it is blown and do whatever you beckon." She handed the vest to the youngest and said, "You will become invisible when you wear this. No one will be able to see you."

The widow explained how the treasures came into the possession of the family and told some stories about how they had been used by various ancestors. "Now that you know how precious they are, I hope you will take good care of them and pass them on to your children," she said. "And remember, do not tell anyone about them or show them to anyone. For anyone who hears about them, will surely covet them."

It was not long before the widow fell ill and died. And not long after the funeral, the two oldest brothers began to brag about their treasures. The youngest reminded them of their mother's warning but they laughed at him and boasted even more.

Word of the brothers' treasures traveled in every direction and soon reached the ears of a greedy princess. She quickly decided that she must have them and schemed how to obtain them.

A few days later she sent a retainer to the oldest brother with an invitation to visit her in her palace. He quickly dressed in his best clothes, stowed the marble carefully inside his vest, and left with the retainer.

The Princess welcomed him in a grand manner. He was served every imaginable delicacy and entertained by beautiful dancers and musicians. He became intoxicated with the sights and the princess's flattery. Finally, when the entertainers left and he found himself alone with the Princess, he took the marble from inside his vest and said, "I have something to show you, Your Highness. I think you will find it very interesting. Watch." He rolled the marble across the floor and, of course, it left a trail of coins.

"It's marvelous!" cried the Princess. "Do it again! Do it again!"

The brother rolled it again and again as the Princess laughed hysterically. Then, suddenly, she grabbed the marble and hid it in her dress. "It's mine now. And so are you," she shouted and before he knew what was happening he was led off to a stockade.

The next day she sent a retainer with an invitation to the second brother. He too was delighted to receive the invitation and quickly left, taking his magic flute in hopes of impressing the princess with it.

The Princess welcomed him as she had his brother. And he was served an elaborate feast and entertained with singing and dancing. He was enthralled with the Princess's flattery.

Wishing to impress her, he said, "I have a flute that Your Highness will find more interesting than any those musicians play."

"Oh? Please show me. I would love to see it," she said excitedly.

"Only when we are alone," said the brother.

"Then I will send everyone away at once," cried the Princess.

When they were finally alone, the brother took his flute from inside his vest. "This is a magic flute. If I blow it, a band of soldiers will appear and do whatever I command."

"How wonderful. Please let me try it," said the Princess demurely, reaching for the flute.

"Of course, Your Highness," said the brother, smiling broadly.

The Princess put the flute to her lips and blew. A band of soldiers appeared before them. With a hideous laugh, she shouted, "Lock this man up!" And so the second brother was dragged off, kicking and shouting.

As for the youngest brother, he worried about his brothers because he thought that it was strange for the Princess, who was known to be very cunning and avaricious, to invite them to the palace and because they had not returned. Finally, he set off for the palace, passing the Princess's retainer on the way. On arriving there, he put on his vest and slipped inside unnoticed. Cautiously he crept throughout the palace in search of his brothers.

Finally, he came to the Princess's room. He watched as she played with the marble and counted the coins it produced, laughing hideously all the while. The sight made him so angry, he struck the wall.

"Who's there?" called the Princess, hiding the marble and the flute under the thick mat on which she was sitting. "That's strange," she said, looking around the room. "I must be hearing things."

A few moments later the brother tried to get the treasures out from under the mat but in his hurry brushed against the Princess.

"Help! Help!" cried the Princess. Guards rushed into the room and looked around perplexed. The brother sneaked out, trying very hard not to brush against any of the guards, as the Princess told them over and over that someone was in her room. He rushed through the palace and out the gate.

Out of breath, he sat down beside a spring to rest. As he pondered what to do, he began to feel hungry. He looked around and spotted a grove of apple trees. He picked a large red one and took a bite. It was unusually sweet and juicy. He took another bite and another. But before he was finished, his nose began to feel strange and suddenly it shot out from his face until the tip was an arm's length away.

"Oh no! What shall I do? What shall I do?" he exclaimed over and over. And as he did, he unconsciously plucked and ate a yellow apple. With each bite his nose shrank until it was back to normal.

"How odd!" he said, gazing at the apples. Then he began to laugh. "I'll teach that greedy Princess a lesson she will never forget." Quickly he picked an armful of apples, wrapped them in his vest, and set off for the village at the entrance to the palace.

In the village, he bought a basket and some clothes and dressed up as a peddler. "Apples! Apples! Juicy, red, delicious apples!" he shouted over and over as he walked around the palace.

It wasn't long before the Princess came outside the gate.

"Apples! Apples! Juicy, red, delicious apples!" he shouted as he walked toward her.

The sight of the glossy red apples made the Princess's mouth water. True to her greedy ways, she bought the entire basket. The brother couldn't help laughing as he watched her go back inside the palace.

Quickly he put on his vest and slipped through the palace gate. Carefully he made his way to the Princess's room. He arrived just in time to see her nose shoot out like an arrow.

"My nose! My nose!" she shouted. "Something is wrong

with my nose!" Maids and guards came running to see what was wrong but each one burst into laughter.

Carefully the brother crept into the room which was quickly filling up with people, slid the treasures out from under the mat, and made his way out again. Then he blew the flute to call forth a band of soldiers and, with their help, soon located his brothers and fled the palace.

The brothers kept their treasures a secret after that and lived long, prosperous lives. As for the Princess, she lived a long sad life with an arrow-like nose to remind her of her greediness.

Cleverness and Stupidity

Shade Selling

It was a blistering hot day. A young man, feeling like he was broiling, looked across the field where he was working at a large zelkova tree in the distance. Smiling broadly, he started walking toward the tree which stood a few steps from the gate of a large house.

The young man was surprised to find a very well-dressed old man asleep on a rush mat under the tree. Not wanting to disturb him, the young man sat down very quietly to rest in the shade with his back against the tree and was soon dozing.

"You rascal! What are you doing sitting in someone else's shade?" screamed the old man.

The young man awoke with a start. "Excuse me. What did you say, Sir?"

"I said what are you doing sitting in someone else's shade!" roared the old man.

The young man looked puzzled. "Someone else's shade? What do you mean 'someone else's' shade?"

"This is my shade!" screamed the old man. "Get out!"

"But this tree belongs to all the villagers," said the young man.

The old man snorted. "My grandfather's grandfather planted this tree. That makes it mine. Now get away from here!"

"I see," said the young man, nodding and smiling. "In that case," he said in a serious tone of voice, "would you be interested in selling me its shade?"

"Why sure," chuckled the old man. "I am the owner of the shade. Give me five *nyang* and it is yours."

The young man gave the old man five coins and, smiling broadly, lay down in the shade.

"Who would have thought there would be someone foolish enough to buy the shade of a tree," the old man chuckled to himself as he moved his rush mat to the shade of another tree.

As the sun moved across the sky, the shadow of the tree grew longer and extended into the old man's yard. After a while, the young man stood up and followed the tree's shadow into the yard and sat down.

"What do you mean coming into another man's yard!" roared the old man. "Get out of here you rascal!"

"Why? What's wrong, Sir?" All I'm doing is sitting in the shade you sold me," said the young man.

"Get out you young impudent fool!" roared the old man.

"I think you are the one who should get out. You sold me the shade of that tree so I am entitled to go where its shade extends."

The old man was flabbergasted. He scowled and, muttering under his breath, stomped into his house.

Presently the young man followed the shadow of the tree to the old man's porch and lay down. Before long he stood up, opened the door and walked into the old man's living room.

"Get out! Get out of my house!" screamed the old man. But the young man just smiled and sat down.

When the shadow disappeared, the young man left the house and went home.

The next day and the next, day after day the young man followed the shade of the tree into the old man's house.

Then one day the old man spoke to the young man in a subdued voice. "Please return the shade of the tree to me. I'll give you back your five *nyang*."

"I wouldn't think of returning this nice shade," replied the young man. "Now get out of it."

The old man could not go anywhere in the village without people pointing and laughing at him. The villagers called him "Greedy Old Shade Seller." "Do you have any shade for us?" they would jeer.

Finally, the old man and his family could not stand it any longer. They left the village in the middle of the night and were never heard of again.

The young man thus found himself the owner of the big house and he let everyone rest under the big zelkova tree beside his gate.

A Trip to Hell and Back

There was once a man who owed a lot of money to a petty government official who was stingy and conniving. The official was always defaming the man and often sent a servant to his house to harangue him about the debt.

Finally, the poor man said to his wife, "I have been thinking that we will never be able to pay the official what we owe him. But I think I know a way to get out of paying it. Now listen carefully. His servant will probably come around again in a few days and this is what I want you to do...."

Indeed, the servant came the next day. He was surprised to hear loud crying coming from inside the house and was even more surprised to see the woman's hair in disarray when she came out to meet him with her small child in her arms.

"What's the matter? Has something happened?" he asked.

"It's my husband. He's dead. He died before the cock crowed of a stomachache brought on by eating cold rice. It's all my fault. It was all I had to feed him when he came home late last night. Oh, what am I to do? I have this small child and...Oh, what am I to do?" the woman fell over sobbing.

The servant peeked inside the house and saw what looked like a body covered with blankets. "I'm very sorry," he said and left.

"Well, did you get any money out of that no good bastard?" asked the official when the servant appeared before him.

"No, Sir, I couldn't. He's dead."

"Dead? Did you say dead?"

"Yes, Sir. He died last night from eating cold rice. His wife was very distraught."

The official clicked his tongue and waved the servant out.

A week later the poor man appeared in the official's office.

"What is the meaning of this? I heard you were dead," said the official, looking a bit confused. "You don't even look like you've been sick."

"I was dead," explained the poor man. "But I returned to this world after three days."

"How could that be?" asked the official. "And where were you?"

"Well, I hate to admit it, but I was in Hell. As soon as I breathed my last breath, a ghost took me by the hand and escorted me there. He took me before the Great King of the Underworld and told me to bow down. I did and then the Great King checked some kind of list and told me I must return to the world of the living, that apparently someone had made a mistake. I told him I didn't know my way back so he told a ghost to escort me.

"As we were going down a crowded street, someone grabbed my hand and said over and over he was glad to see me. At first I didn't recognize him because he was dressed rather shabbily and was wearing a bamboo hat instead of a horsehair one. I just stared at him and he said 'Don't you know me, I'm...'"

"Well, who was it? Was it someone I also know?" asked the official.

"Well, yes," hesitated the poor man. "It was your father."

"You saw my father?" asked the official excitedly.

"Yes, I saw him. He looked very destitute. I asked him what he was doing there beside the road. He said that he was so poor he had no where to stay and that he was surviving on scraps. He asked about you and the rest of your family. I told him and then we cried together. I found a coin in my vest pocket and gave it to him. I wished I could give him more, but it was all I had. Then the ghost hurried me away."

"Did you happen to see my mother?" the official asked in a low voice.

"Yes, I did but I think you would prefer not to hear about her. It's rather embarrassing...and...well..."

"No. Please tell me. We are the only ones here. Please speak freely."

"Well, after a while the ghost said he was thirsty so we stopped in a tavern for a bowl of wine. It was a noisy, bawdy place but the wine was good. And, it's hard to tell you this, the owner was your mother. She looked very happy and wealthy. She recognized me before I recognized her. She seemed very happy to see me and treated me and my guide to a large feast. She asked all about you and your family. I told her what I could."

"That's odd," said the official. "If she is so wealthy that she can own a tavern, why is Father homeless and poor?"

The poor man was silent. "Tell me. I'm sure you know," the official repeated over and over.

Finally the poor man spoke. "It is not easy for me to tell you this. I wish I didn't have to but if you insist on knowing....Your mother and your father could not get along....They stopped living together.... And now...well... your mother lives with my father. I was shocked at first. But they seem to love and respect each other very much." He paused and then said, "I didn't want to tell you."

The official's face turned scarlet and then pale. He stared into space for a while and finally said in a very low voice, "Don't ever tell anyone about this. If my parents' situation is ever revealed, I will never be able to hold up my head."

"You don't need to worry. I would never breathe a word to anyone. You have my word."

"Thank you. It would ruin me. And, about the debt you owe me, you can consider it paid. And, please visit my home often."

The poor man excused himself and left. He chuckled to himself all the way home.

He and his family visited the official's home frequently thereafter and were always treated to a sumptuous banquet. They were also provided financial help whenever needed.

Umbrellas and Straw Shoes

There once was a woman who was constantly worrying about her two sons who were peddlers. The oldest sold umbrellas and the youngest, straw shoes. One day after the long rainy season had ended, a neighbor stopped in to say hello. "Don't you feel great now that the rainy season is finally over," she greeted the woman.

"Well, I don't know. It just makes me worry."

"What do you mean it makes you worry?"

"Well, as you know, my oldest son sells umbrellas. So, with the weather like this, I'm afraid he won't be able to sell any."

On a rainy day a week or so later, the neighbor stopped in again. "After all those scorching hot days, isn't this rain nice? It has certainly cooled things down a lot," she said with a smile. "Don't you feel better now?"

"No, not at all," replied the woman glumly. "The rain just makes me worry."

"But why do you have to worry?" asked the neighbor.

"Because my second son sells straw shoes. Do you think anyone will buy any now that the ground is so muddy?"

The neighbor shook her head back and forth and smiled. "So, you worry when it rains, and you worry when it doesn't."

"Yes, that's right. I want both of my sons to do well. So how can I not worry?"

The two women were silent for a while. Then the neighbor slapped her knee. "I know how to solve your problem. You just do what I say and then you won't have to worry. Now listen. When it's cloudy or rainy, just say to yourself, 'Oh, how nice! My first son should be able to sell lots of umbrellas.' And, when it's nice and sunny, just say, 'Oh, how nice! My second son should be able to sell lots of straw shoes.' You see, you have always thought negatively, not positively. From now on you should look at the bright side of things. If you think that way, then you won't have to worry."

"Why that's true. I have always looked at the bad side of things. From now on I'm going to look at the bright."

And in that way the woman learned the power of positive thinking and was forever happy.

Winter Strawberries

T here was a wealthy, ill-natured man who took great pleasure in harassing his servants. Then one cold winter day he called a manservant to his study and said, "These days I don't feel very good. I think my body could do with some strawberries. Go pick some and bring them to me."

"Begging your pardon, Sir, but what you ask is impossible. Strawberries don't grow in winter," said the servant.

"How dare you say my request is impossible?" stormed the master. "Haven't you ever heard of the man who dug bamboo shoots in the snow to feed his parents? You should serve your master as you would your parents! Now go but be sure you bring me some strawberries tomorrow!"

The servant knew that his master was terribly stubborn and unreasonable but he could not help feeling sad and embarrassed at being openly rebuked by him. With a heavy heart he trudged home through the thick snow, knowing that he would have to face him empty-handed the next day and no doubt be punished.

"Daddy! Daddy! What's wrong?" cried his young son. "You look as if you can hardly walk. What's the matter?"

"Nothing. Nothing," said the servant, shaking his head as he went inside and sat down. Then he told his wife what had happened.

"Don't worry, Father," said the boy, after listening to his

father and mother talk. "I will go see the master tomorrow and talk to him. I will tell him something that will make everything all right. Just get some rest. There's nothing to worry about."

Hearing this, the servant and his wife just smiled and they all three lay down and went to sleep.

The next morning the young boy slipped out of the house before his parents had a chance to protest and went to the big house.

"What are you doing here?" snarled the master. "Did you bring the strawberries I ordered your father to get?"

The boy lowered his head. "Yesterday my father went up the mountain to look for strawberries," he said, letting his voice trail off.

"Well where the hell are they?" shouted the master.

"He got bit by a poisonous snake so he's home in bed," said the boy.

"Why you impudent little bastard! What kind of fool do you take me for?" screeched the master. "Everyone knows that snakes don't come out in winter! It's too cold!"

"Then, Sir," said the boy in a very loud voice, "If there are no snakes in winter, how can there be strawberries?"

The master's mouth fell open and his face went scarlet. He turned and without a word retreated into his study. Needless to say that from then the master did not make any silly demands of his servants.

The Trial of the Stone Statue

One autumn day, a long time ago, a silk salesman was returning home to Ch'ŏnan with a load of silk he had purchased in Hanyang. When he reached the top of the Kwach'ŏn pass, he looked around for a place to rest and spotted a grave with a stone guardian figure in front of it. He took the load of silk off his back, carefully placed it on the ground beside the stone statue, and sat down with his back against the statue.

"I should be able to make a big profit with this silk," the salesman told himself. "The color, the sheen, the feel are so excellent no one will argue about the price. I should be able to pay off what I owe and get something for the wife and kids." He smiled and looked contentedly at the high blue sky as he daydreamed. Soon his head began to bob and in no time he was fast asleep.

After a while, the salesman opened his eyes with a start. "What am I doing? This is no time to sleep," he said, rubbing the sleep from his eyes. "I better get on home and get this silk sold."

He stood up, stretched, straightened his clothes, brushed the dust off the seat of his pants, and turned to pick up the bundle of silk. "That's strange. I'm sure I put the silk down here." He looked on the other side of the statue. He walked around the grave. The silk had vanished.

"It can't be! It can't be!" cried the salesman and he began

to run down the trail, looking to the left and right. "I've got to find that thief! I've got to!" He said over and over as thoughts of what would happen if he didn't swirled in his head.

Presently he came to a village. He walked up and down every alley. "Have you seen anyone with a large bundle of silk? I've been robbed!" He called to everyone he met.

Finally, tired and exhausted, he slumped down on the ground beside a large tree and wept, all the time blabbering to himself about his troubles and the loss of his fortune.

"What's the matter?" asked an old man. "Why are you crying?"

"Well, I was on my way home with a load of silk..." explained the salesman. "So you see, I've got to find that silk. If I don't, my family will be ruined."

"Yes, you do have a problem," said the sympathetic old man. He stroked his beard a few times and said, "What you should do is go ask our Magistrate for help. He is very good at solving problems. He is very kind. I'm sure if you ask him to find the thief, he will."

"Do you really think he would help me?" asked the salesman.

"Yes, I believe he will. Come on, I'll take you to him," said the old man.

The salesman told the Magistrate his story and asked him to help find the thief.

The Magistrate was silent for a few minutes, during which time the people in the room mumbled among themselves that this was a case he wouldn't be able to solve. Finally, he said, "You're sure there was no one around when you lost the silk?"

"Yes, Your Honor, I'm sure. I looked all around the area where I was and, since I was at the top of the pass, I could see a long way in every direction. There wasn't anyone in

sight."

"And you didn't meet anyone on the trail coming or going?"

"That's right."

"And tell me again exactly where you were and what you were doing when the theft occurred."

"I was leaning against a stone statue of a guard. It was in front of a grave. I put my silk on the ground beside it and sat down to rest with my back against it and fell asleep."

"So, the statue must have seen everything," said the Magistrate to everyone's astonishment. "We must question the statue."

"But, Your Honor," said the salesman, "the statue isn't a man. It is made of stone."

"Hush! The statue is our only clue!" shouted the Magistrate. Turning to his guards, he said, "Bring in the statue for questioning!" The guards' eyes grew big and they stood motionless. "What are you standing around for! I told you to bring in that statue! Now go! Follow this man to the place and bring the statue in at once!"

"But, Sir, a statue can't..."

"I gave you an order! Now do it!"

The guards followed the salesman to the grave, all the while discussing the sanity of the Magistrate. They dug up the statue, bound it with a rope, and carried it back to the Magistrate.

By the time they returned, news of the Magistrate's bizarre actions had spread throughout the town. A throng of people followed the guards to the Magistrate's office.

A guard called for silence as the Magistrate began the questioning. "There's no doubt that you saw the salesman place his bundle of silk on the ground, that you saw him fall asleep, and that you saw someone take his bundle of silk," said the Magistrate sternly. "Now tell me who took the silk."

All was silent except for a few muffled laughs that came from the crowd.

"Why don't you answer me? You must know what happened to the silk. Now tell me! Who took the silk?"

Laughter rippled through the crowd of onlookers. The Magistrate called for silence. "I know how to make you talk," he stormed, staring at the statue. "Guards, whip it!"

The guards began flailing the statue with sticks. "Harder! Harder!" The Magistrate yelled at the guards. "Hit it until it talks!"

The onlookers could not keep from laughing any longer. They burst into loud guffaws.

"What is the meaning of this!" stormed the Magistrate.

"How dare you interrupt this trial! Guards, arrest these people! Throw them all in the stockade! Now!"

"Wait!" "Wait!" "Have mercy!" cried the people.

"Please, Your Honor," said a man, stepping out of the crowd. "We meant no wrong. It's just that the thought of a stone statue speaking is rather comical. Please, Your Honor. Please have mercy on us."

"I admit that this is a rather bizarre case. However, I am trying to solve it in the only lawful way I know how. And you interrupted the trial by laughing at me. It is a disgrace," said the Magistrate sternly. "Still, I will give you all a second chance. You can go free. But, within four days, each of you must bring me a roll of silk. Anyone who doesn't bring a roll of silk will be punished."

Four days later a long line of people carrying rolls of silk formed in the yard of the Magistrate's office. The Magistrate had them put the rolls of silk in a pile. He looked closely at the rolls and even his untrained eyes could see that many of them were of the same high quality. "Look closely at those rolls of silk and tell me if any are like the ones you lost," he told the salesman.

The salesman examined the rolls of silk. He put a number of them in a pile and said, "These are just like the ones I lost."

"Well, I am going to give them to you because I believe they are yours," said the Magistrate. "Now count them and tell me if all of the rolls you had are there."

Smiling for the first time in days, the salesman counted the rolls. "Three are missing. But I don't mind. I'm just happy to get this many back."

"Nonsense! We must find the other three," said the Magistrate. "Would the people who brought these rolls of silk step forward." A group of people shuffled forward. "Where did you get those rolls of silk?"

"Your Honor, all of us worked together to get them. We asked everyone we knew and everyone who passed through. We finally heard that there was a silk salesman at a tavern in the village on the other side of the mountain. We sent someone there to buy some silk for all of us," explained one of the group.

The Magistrate ordered some guards to go to the tavern and arrest the man. They returned with an unkempt man. On his back was the rest of the bundle he had stolen from the salesman.

The Magistrate growled at the man. "You bastard, I know that you stole this man's silk while he sat against that statue dozing. We've recovered all but three rolls. Where are they?"

The thief gestured toward the bundle on his back.

"Guards give the bundle to the salesman and lock this thief up." The Magistrate was silent for a while. Then he apologized to the townspeople, thanked them for their help and returned the money they had paid the thief for the silk. The salesman thanked everyone and happily set out down the trail for home.

The Magistrate became even more famous as news of the stone statue's trial spread throughout the land.

Catching Tigers with a Greased Puppy

I n a certain hollow, in the olden times, there was a kind,
hard working young man. He and his older brother
shared everything equally after the death of their
parents, but his greedy brother eventually took everything
from him. The villagers felt sorry for him so they gave him
an abandoned plot of land on the mountain behind the
village.

He worked very hard to prepare the land to plant rice
and barley, but it was too rocky so he decided to try to
grow sesame. However, he didn't have the money to buy
the seeds so, after much thought, he went to his brother
and asked him for some seeds.

"Where do you plan to plant the seeds?" asked the older
brother.

"A plot of land the villagers loaned me. Please give me
some seeds. I'll repay you with sesame oil after my first
harvest."

The older brother was angered by the news that the villagers had provided his brother with a plot of land. But,
with a smile, he told him to wait for him to bring the seeds.
After a while he returned, grinning broadly, with a bag of
seeds. Once his brother was out the gate, he burst into laughter because he had boiled the seeds.

Happily the young man planted the seeds and anxiously
waited for sprouts to push through the topsoil. Fortunately, one sprout finally did; undoubtedly it was the only seed

that had not been boiled.

The plant's growth was miraculous. It produced new stems overnight and grew so large that it became the talk of the village. By autumn it covered the whole plot of land and was loaded with fist-size seed pods.

The young man worked hard all day to harvest the seeds. Then, without taking a rest, he began pressing them because he wanted to repay his brother as soon as possible. He worked late into the night to press the oil. He filled a large jar to take him the next day and happily went to sleep.

The next morning he was astonished to find the jar empty. But soon discovered that a stray puppy which had taken up with him had eaten the oil. He was furious.

"You worthless mutt! I'll feed you to the tigers!" he shouted. He quickly tied a rope around the puppy and led him into the forest.

He went deep into the forest until he came to a spot where tigers had been sighted many times. It was near a large cave. He tied the puppy to a tree and left.

It wasn't long before a large tiger caught the puppy's scent. It took the puppy into its big mouth but the puppy was so slippery from the oil it slid right down the tiger's throat. The sesame oil had a laxative effect and the puppy soon slid out the tiger's anus.

Presently another tiger appeared and greedily took the puppy in its mouth. But the same thing happened; the puppy slid right down its throat and out its anus. One tiger after another ate the puppy with the same result.

Later in the day, the young man felt remorseful for what he had done to the puppy. Hoping it was still alive, he went to retrieve it. He was astounded to find that the puppy was not only alive, but sleeping at the end of a string of tigers.

He rushed back to the village for help. And, with the aid of several friends, he killed the tigers and sold their skins

for a hefty sum of money.

He shared his wealth with the villagers and loved the puppy as he would a friend.

The Tiger and the Coal Peddler's Wife

D eep in the mountains lived a young couple who supported themselves by digging and selling coal. It was a hard life and a lonely one for their nearest neighbor was thirty *ri* away. Still they were very happy and anxiously awaited the birth of their first child, which was due any time.

Early one morning the man headed out to the nearest village, where it was market day, to sell a load of coal and buy some supplies. However, because of a sudden rainstorm, there were not many shoppers so he went from one remote house to another peddling his coal. By the time he had sold all of it and returned to the village to buy the much needed supplies, it was too late for him to return home.

Meanwhile, his wife gave birth. And, ironically, their dog gave birth to three puppies.

The woman lay in bed, cuddling the baby and dozing. It became dusk and she began to worry. Knowing she must eat something to be able to nurse the baby, she got up out of bed and began preparing seaweed soup.

She heard something outside and, thinking it was her husband, threw open the door and found herself staring into the eyes of a very large tiger.

She was overcome with fear but, thinking of her newborn baby, she tried to stay calm. Out of the corner of her eye she saw the puppies. "Here's some meat for you!" she shouted, grabbing up one of them and tossing it out the door.

The tiger caught the puppy in its mouth, gulped it down and looked at the woman hungrily.

"Here! Take this!" she shouted, throwing it another puppy.

The tiger gulped it down and stared at the woman.

She looked at her faithful dog and its remaining puppy. She couldn't bring herself to give the puppy to the tiger. Glancing around she noticed some cotton. She quickly wrapped it around a hot coal from the cooking fire and tossed it to the tiger.

As with the puppies, the tiger caught it in its mouth and quickly gulped it down. Its eyes became big and it opened its mouth as though choking. It ran a few steps this way and that. Then it fell forward on its front legs and then over on its side. The woman watched its body shake and become still.

Her husband returned home early the next morning and was alarmed to see a dead tiger in front of his house. But his alarm turned to relief when his wife met him at the door with their newborn son in her arms.

The man sold the tiger skin for a lot of money and from then on they lived more comfortably.

The Mad Magistrate

In Honam* in the olden days there was a very ill-tempered magistrate of bad judgment. The townspeople were afraid of him and did not always agree with the laws he enforced. In fact, many people had begun to move away because of what he was doing to the town and many of his staff had begun to worry about what was happening.

Then one day the chief secretary called a meeting of all the Magistrate's office staff and guards. "I think that most of you are of the same opinion as I am about our Magistrate. Something must be done. His severe rule and snap judgments will lead to catastrophe if something is not done. We must think of a way to get rid of him. Does anyone have a good idea?"

They discussed various ideas and finally one of them said, "I just thought of the perfect scheme. Let's do this. One of..."

They all agreed that it was worth trying and discussed the details and what role each person would play.

Several days passed before the opportune time for them to put their plan into action came. The Magistrate was not conducting business and only the office staff were present. Without a word, a clerk walked up to the Magistrate and slapped him on the face.

"What is the meaning of this?" screamed the Magistrate.

---

*Honam: the southern region comprising the provinces of Chŏllabuk-do and Chŏllanam-do.

"Guards, arrest this man at once!" But the guards didn't move.

"Are you deaf! I said arrest this man!" screamed the Magistrate. "He slapped my face! Arrest the bastard!"

No one moved but they said in loud whispers, "The Magistrate must be ill. Why else would he accuse someone of slapping his face?"

"You idiots! Are you blind as well? This man slapped my face!" screamed the Magistrate, pointing at the clerk.

Everyone stood still and looked confused. "Damn you! Damn you all! I'll have you all thrown in the stockade!" screamed the Magistrate as he kicked over his desk. He stomped to the door and yelled, "Guards! Guards!"

One of the clerks went to the Magistrate's residence to inform his family. "The Honorable Magistrate appears to be ill," he told the Magistrate's wife and sons. "He will not let anyone help him. And...well...forgive me for saying this, it seems like he has gone mad. I think you should come talk to him. Maybe he'll listen to you."

The Magistrate's family rushed to his office. The Magistrate looked mad indeed. His face was scarlet, his nostrils were flaring, and, because he had been shouting and screaming constantly, his mouth was frothy. "That insolent bastard slapped me!" he pointed and shouted as soon as he saw his sons. "The bastard slapped me and..." The Magistrate explained what had happened.

The sons thought that he had fallen ill because they did not believe anyone, especially a staff member, would be so bold as to slap the Magistrate. "Please calm down, Father," said the oldest son. "You must get hold of yourself."

"Please come home with us," said the second son. "We'll call a doctor for you."

"You fools, I'm not sick! This man slapped me, I tell you."

"Now, Father, you really don't expect us to believe a clerk

struck you," said the oldest son in a soft voice. "A clerk may not be very smart or have very good manners but surely he wouldn't slap you."

"You're no better than the rest of them!" screamed the Magistrate, pounding his desk with his fist. "Get out! Get out of my sight!"

The sons left the room and spoke with some of the staff. Presently they had a doctor brought in.

When the doctor entered the Magistrate's chambers, the Magistrate waved him out, shouting over and over, "Out! Out! I'm not sick! There's not a thing wrong with me!"

The Magistrate spent the rest of the day screaming at his staff and anyone else who entered his chambers. That evening he screamed at his wife and sons and he couldn't eat or sleep.

His behavior and appearance became worse every day. Everyone, with the exception of those involved in the scheme, thought that his behavior was the result of an illness that had befallen him.

News of the Magistrate's illness spread quickly and soon the Governor heard about his trouble. He retired him and appointed a new magistrate.

On his way to his hometown, the Magistrate stopped at the Governor's office to pay his respects. "I was sorry to hear about your sudden illness. I hope you are feeling better," said the Governor.

"I feel fine. There's not a thing wrong with me. It was just that being slapped by..."

"Now, now, don't get excited," interrupted the Governor. "I think you should hurry home, it seems like you might have a relapse."

The Magistrate sadly journeyed to his hometown. And until his death, many years later, he could not bring up the incident without his family saying his illness had returned.

Three Brothers' Inheritance

A long time ago in a certain village there lived three brothers who were very devoted to their father. They were very poor and what little they earned went to buy medicine for their father who had been sick for many years.

One day he called them to his bedside. "I think the time to discard my spoon and chopsticks is near," he said in a raspy voice and began coughing. "I don't have much," he continued when the coughing spell was over, "but please share everything."

He died the next day and the brothers buried him beside their mother's tomb on a nearby mountain. Sadly the brothers discarded his spoon and chopsticks and divided up their inheritance—a stick, a drum and three hollow gourds. The oldest took the stick, the second oldest, the drum, and the youngest, the gourds.

A few days later the oldest said, "I've been thinking we should go out into the world and seek our fortunes. We can each go a separate way. But we should meet back here a year later for Father's *chesa** since we will have to prepare the memorial table."

They all agreed and the next day began their quest. The

---

* *Chesa:* an ancestral memorial service involving the offering of special foods and bows by families on the anniversary of a person's birth and death.

oldest brother took a road that led into the foothills. He walked all day and when the sun went down he realized he should find a place to stay the night. He walked for a long time but could not see a house anywhere. Finally, he came upon a cluster of tombs and quickly decided he would sleep between two of them. He made a mound of leaves and grass and then wiggled his way into it and fell asleep.

In the middle of the night he was awakened by the sound of voices. Thinking they might belong to bandits, he lay very still.

"Do you smell something strange?"

"Yes," replied a hoarse voice. "I can't recall what it is but I'm sure I've smelled it before."

"It seems to be coming from here," came the first voice from near the oldest brother's feet.

The oldest brother tried to squint to see but his eyes popped open at the sight of two ghosts.

"Who are you?" asked the tallest ghost. "I've never seen you before."

"Oh, I was just put here today," said the oldest brother, trying to be calm.

"But you don't look like a ghost," said the tall ghost. "Show me your arm!"

The oldest brother stuck out the slender end of his stick. "Hmm... Show me your leg," said the short ghost.

The oldest brother stuck out the thick end of his stick.

Apparently satisfied, the two ghosts sat down a few steps away and began talking.

"Well, I guess we can count on snatching a pretty young spirit in a day or so," chuckled the tall ghost.

"What do you mean?" asked the short one.

"You know that big house in the village east of here. Well the only daughter there is sick and no one knows how to cure her. She would be fine if they would give her some mugwort tea."

"Their loss is our gain," laughed the short ghost and the tall one laughed too.

A cock crowed in the distance and the ghosts immediately disappeared. When it became light enough to see, the oldest brother set off toward the east, hoping it wasn't too late to save the sick girl.

The rich man was so shocked to hear that a young man claiming he could cure his sick daughter was at the gate that he agreed to meet him. He and his wife were so impressed with the oldest brother's self-confidence that they agreed to let him try to cure her and ordered the servants to do whatever he said.

The oldest brother had the servants bring as much mugwort as they could. He then boiled it with water and spooned the liquid into the girl's mouth. Within minutes the young girl sat up and looked around the room as if she were just waking up from a long nap.

Overjoyed at seeing his daughter well again, the man immediately offered the oldest brother her hand in marriage. The oldest brother consented and as a wedding gift received half of the man's wealth and property.

Meanwhile, the second brother was making his way through the mountains. As he was passing through a village he noticed a large gathering of people and stopped to see what was going on. "What's all the fuss about?" he asked one of the villagers.

"Just take a look at that notice," replied the man.

The second brother squeezed through the crowd. "A reward of half of this village is offered for the capture of the man-eating tiger that has been preying on this village," he read excitedly.

"Where does the tiger live?" he asked the people around him.

"It lives in the mountain just over those three knolls," said an old man, pointing toward the west. "I can see you're not from around here. You best be careful. That bastard has terrorized us for months. I don't know how many people he has..."

The second brother thanked the old man and set off toward the west. He finally reached the mountain and, after a short rest, headed deep into the forest. He examined the trees as he walked and eventually climbed up one which towered above some large rocks and, knowing the wind would carry his scent through the forest, waited for the tiger.

It wasn't long before he saw the tiger slinking through the forest. It sniffed around the foot of the tree and then looked up at the second brother. With a loud growl, it began climbing the tree.

Holding his drum tightly, the second brother watched as the tiger climbed higher and higher. *Kkung! Kkung! Kkung!* he struck the drum as hard as he could. The startled tiger fell to its death on the rocks below.

The second brother made a frame of sticks and dragged the tiger back to the village to claim his reward. The villagers celebrated with feasting and dancing. The village leader gave the second brother his due reward and also offered him his daughter's hand in marriage. He consented and within a few days was happily married.

Meanwhile, the youngest brother was making his way through the mountains in the opposite direction. One late afternoon he spotted a house in the distance and decided to ask to spend the night there. He quickened his steps and arrived there as the sun was going down.

"Hello! Hello!" he called but there was no response even though he could hear someone. He walked into the yard and was surprised to see a young woman with tears streaming down her face throwing dishes onto the ground. "Hello!" he called out. "Don't be startled. I'm just a wayfarer who needs a place to spend the night. And, by the way, why are you breaking those dishes?"

"Oh, please, please help me," she cried. "There's a two-headed monster that lives in that forest. It has eaten all of my family and tonight it is coming for me." She picked up a dish and threw it down on the ground. "I'm breaking these dishes to try to scare it away."

"Don't worry," said the youngest brother, "I'll help you. Just let me think."

After a while he told her to go to sleep. Presently he lay down beside her and pulled a quilt up to his neck. Then he put one of his gourds over his face and held one on each side of his head. In the unlighted room, he looked like he had three heads.

In the middle of the night, he heard heavy footsteps coming through the yard. He tried to lay perfectly still as he heard them approaching the door. He felt a burst of cold air as the door opened.

The monster stuck one head in the open door and looked around. Then it quickly closed the door and whispered, "We've got trouble. That girl is sleeping with a three-headed man."

"Nonsense," said the other head. "There's no such thing as a three-headed man."

"I'm telling you I saw it with these two eyes. It didn't have a single hair on its heads. It must be very smart, being so old. We better get out of here."

"We're not going anywhere until I have a look with my own eyes." So the monster pushed open the door and stuck in his other head.

The youngest brother banged the gourds together and yelled, "Stop you filthy bastard! You move a step and you're dead!"

"Please don't kill me!" cried the monster. Please forgive me! Please let me go!"

"After what you've done to this poor woman's family, I should slay you on the spot. But I'm going to let you go. But you must bring me all your treasures before this night is over. And if you ever do this kind of thing again, I promise I'll kill you. That you can count on."

"All right! All right! Whatever you say!" begged the monster. "Just don't kill me!"

"Go!" screamed the youngest brother. "And put all your treasures in the yard beside the well!"

Although very frightened, the youngest brother opened the door slightly and watched the monster make several trips into the forest to bring his treasures. "That's all I have," the monster's voice suddenly shattered the stillness, startling the youngest brother.

"Then get out of here!" shouted the youngest brother.

When the sun came up the youngest brother and the woman went outside to see what the monster had left. They were surprised to see a great pile of gold, silver and precious gems.

The youngest brother asked the woman to be his wife and much to his happiness, she consented.

On the anniversary of their father's death, the three brothers returned home as they had promised. They happily told their stories and congratulated each other. They held the memorial service for their father and visited his grave. They erected a large stone marker and each one said a special thank you as he made the customary two bows in front of the tomb.

For the Love of Honey

I n a certain mountain village there was once a small private school led by a very strict teacher. As the students recited their lessons or practiced their calligraphy, he would stealthily eat something from a jar he kept in a small chest beside his desk. It was a constant source of curiosity for the young boys.

One day, one of the students said, "Sŏnsaengnim,* what are you eating? It seems like it must be very good."

"No. No. It's not good. It's medicine," said the teacher.

"Are you sick?" cried the boys.

"No. Don't worry," laughed the teacher. "It's just something to make me strong. But you mustn't eat any. It would kill you."

All the students but the most clever and bright one believed him.

A few days later the teacher said that he had to go out for a short time to attend a banquet and for the students to practice their writing until he returned.

As soon as he was sure the teacher was gone, the clever boy opened the teacher's small chest to find out what he was constantly eating.

"What are you doing?" said one of the boys.

"You're going to get us all in trouble!" said another.

---

*Sŏnsaengnim: literally meaning teacher, the word is also used as a term of respect.

"*Sŏnsaengnim* will beat you for sure!" said another.

"You fools! Why should he beat me? He lied to us. That's worse," explained the clever boy as he placed the jar on the teacher's desk. "Here, see for yourselves. This isn't medicine. It's honey," he said, dipping his fingers into the jar and licking them.

The other boys quickly scrambled to get a hand in the jar. Happily they dipped and licked their fingers until it was empty. Then they suddenly became silent as the thought of what they had done began to sink in.

"What do you think will happen when *Sŏnsaengnim* finds the jar empty?" one of the boys said nervously.

"Don't worry. Just do what I say," said the clever boy.

"Do you have a plan?" asked one of the boys.

"Yes. But it is rather mean. Still, since we are his students, I think he'll understand?" And so saying, the clever boy picked up the teacher's ink stone and dropped it on the floor. The other boys stared open-mouthed at the broken ink stone.

"Why did you do that?" the boys shouted at once.

"You'll see," said the clever boy confidently. "Now lay down on the floor. *Sŏnsaengnim* should be returning any minute now. When you hear him coming, moan and groan and roll around on the floor, clutching your stomachs like you're sick. I'll take care of the rest."

The boys lay down to wait, hoping all the time that the clever boy was right. Presently they heard the teacher clear his throat as he always did when he came through the gate to let them know he was approaching.

"Oh, my stomach!" "I'm dying! I'm dying!" "My stomach hurts!" The boys cried over and over, rolling around on the floor.

"What's wrong?" exclaimed the teacher, coming into the room.

"*Sŏnsaengnim*, they're dying," explained the clever boy. "Everyone was playing around and accidentally broke your ink stone. We felt so guilty we ate your medicine to kill ourselves. And now everyone's stomach hurts."

The teacher smiled knowingly at the clever boy and merely said, "All right. Everyone get up. It's time to study our letters."

The teacher never again lied to his students nor secretly ate in their presence. As for the clever boy, he grew up to become a government official famous for his astute judgment.

The Old Woman and the Tiger

In times gone by there was an old woman who lived all by herself in a one-room house at the edge of a forest. Her only means of support was a small bean patch.

One day she looked at her bean patch and shook her head in disgust. It was not the only time that she had found several of the plants destroyed for there was a tiger who came regularly to her patch to feast. "I have got to do something about that tiger," she told herself over and over. Finally, she slapped her knee and smiled. "I know what I'll do," she said and started to clean up the mess the tiger had made.

The next morning the old woman went to the bean patch very early in the hope of seeing the tiger. He was there. The remains of several bean plants lay at his feet.

"Oh, Mr. Tiger," called the old woman from a safe distance. "You must be tired of eating beans all the time. Would you like to come to my house this evening to have red bean porridge? I'm going to make a big batch and you're welcome to have some."

"Red bean porridge?" asked the tiger. "I don't think I know what that is?"

"Well, you'll just have to come try it to see what it is. But I can assure you that there is no way to compare it with those uncooked beans. It is very delicious," said the old woman. "Will you come?"

"Yes, I'll come," said the tiger and he sauntered off into

the forest.

The old woman smiled and giggled as she cleaned up the mess the tiger had made. She quickly pulled out some weeds and then hurried home to prepare for the tiger's visit.

First, she burned some wood in a brazier until only coals remained. Then she put ground red pepper in a large jar of water in the kitchen and stuck every needle she had in a towel and placed it beside the water jar. Then she spread a lot of cow dung outside the kitchen door so that the ground became quite slippery. Finally, she placed a large straw mat on the ground near the cow dung, tied a donkey near the gate, and went inside to wait for the tiger.

The sun was just starting to set when the tiger arrived. "Are you home?" he called as he came through the open gate.

"Welcome! Welcome!" called the old woman as she opened the door. "I'm sorry, but I must ask a favor of you. On your way in, could you please bring me that brazier there by the step."

"Oh, there's no need to feel sorry. After all, you're going to feed me red bean porridge," said the tiger, walking over to the brazier. "The fire is out," he called.

"Oh, well, just blow it. There should be some embers and that will start them burning," said the old woman. "But you have to put your face close to the brazier and blow very hard."

The tiger did as he was told and, of course, ashes flew into the air. "Oh! Oh! My eyes! The ashes went into my eyes!" cried the tiger.

"Oh, that's too bad," said the old woman. "There's a large jar of water in the kitchen. Go in and wash your eyes with the water."

The tiger staggered into the kitchen and splashed water into his eyes. "Oh! Oh! It burns! It burns! My eyes feel like they are on fire!" cried the tiger over and over.

"There's a towel beside the water jar," explained the old woman. "Wipe your eyes with it and you should be all right," she said, struggling to keep from laughing.

The tiger rubbed his eyes with the towel. He howled as the needles stuck his eyes and face. "Oh! It hurts! It hurts! I can't see! She tricked me! She tricked me! I've got to get out of here!" he howled and ran out the kitchen door.

The tiger slipped on the cow dung and fell hard onto the straw mat. The old woman quickly rolled up the mat, bound it with a rope and tied it behind the donkey. Leading the donkey, she dragged the wrapped up tiger to a high cliff and pushed him over the edge. That was the end of the tiger and from then on the old woman's bean patch flourished.

A Wife for a Grain of Millet

A certain young man was traveling to Hanyang, the capital, to take the national *kwagŏ* examination in the hope of receiving a government position. At sundown he stopped at an inn to spend the night.

The innkeeper showed him to a room. "Wait," called the young man as the innkeeper turned to go. "I want you to keep something for me. I'm so tired I'm afraid I wouldn't wake up if someone came in." He took something from his pack and said, "Here, take this grain of millet and keep it in a safe place for me until morning. It means a lot to me. I think it will be safer with you than here."

The innkeeper left, shaking his head and thinking he had let the room to a very strange person. He put the grain of millet in a crack in a corner of the kitchen.

The next morning when the young man asked for the grain of millet, the innkeeper said nonchalantly,"It seems like a rat ate it."

"What? How could you put my grain of millet in a place where a rat could get it? I trusted you to keep it safe!" stormed the young man. "Give me the rat!"

The innkeeper stared at the young man in disbelief and then walked away. Presently he returned with a rat and the young man departed carrying it safely.

That evening when the young man stopped at an inn, he asked the innkeeper to keep the rat safely for him until morning.

The next morning when he asked for the rat, the innkeeper replied, "The cat ate it."

"How could you allow that to happen?" screamed the young man. "It was my property. I entrusted you with it. So now you must give me the cat."

The innkeeper gave the cat to the young man and he set off on his journey.

That night when he put up at an inn he entrusted the cat to the innkeeper. The next morning the innkeeper informed him that a horse had kicked it to death.

"You shouldn't have let that happen," said the young man sternly. "I entrusted you with something of mine and you didn't take care of it properly. So you must give me the horse that destroyed it."

The innkeeper was flabbergasted but he could not argue with the young man's reasoning. So the young man rode off on the horse for Hanyang.

That night he took a room at an inn and asked the innkeeper to take care of his horse. The next morning the innkeeper told him that a bull had gored the horse to death.

As he had done at the other inns, the young man accused the innkeeper of negligence and demanded the bull. The innkeeper consented and the young man departed, driving the bull down the road toward Hanyang.

That night he arrived at an inn on the outskirts of the city. He asked the innkeeper to take care of the bull. The next morning the innkeeper informed him that his son had mistakenly sold the bull. The young man lost his temper and demanded to be taken to the person who had purchased it. The innkeeper refused at first because the buyer was a court minister. He offered the young man another bull but he refused, saying he only wanted to be taken to the man who had bought his bull. The innkeeper finally agreed to take him.

The innkeeper apologized profusely to the Minister and humbly explained why he was there. To his surprise, the Minister said, "I'll see him. With that kind of nerve and determination, he must be interesting."

So the young man was shown into the Minister's study. "I'm here for my bull," he said at once. "Give it to me."

"I wish I could. You see," explained the Minister with a smile, "it's already been killed and eaten."

"Then bring me whoever ate it," said the young man.

The Minister smiled at the young man's words and felt that he must be very clever. "You do have a point," he said, "But of course that is impossible. Instead, I would like to offer you to stay in my home until you take the *kwagŏ*."

The young man accepted the Minister's offer. He passed the *kwagŏ* and the Minister offered him his daughter's hand in marriage. The young man married her and lived a long and prosperous life.

Potpourri

Fire Dogs

Once upon a time there was a place called the King-dom of Darkness. It was pitch black without a smidgen of light anywhere. Its people raised large fierce dogs called fire dogs.

The King of the Kingdom of Darkness fretted very much about the sad state of his country. He wanted it to be bright like other countries.

One day as the King sat thinking about what could be done to bring light to his land, he suddenly slapped his knee and smiled.

"Here boy! Come here!" he called to his fiercest fire dog. "This land is so dark it's hard to live here. Go steal the sun and bring it back here to light our land."

"Yes, my lord. I will go at once and get the sun for you." And with those words, the fire dog flew off like an arrow.

The fire dog flew for several days without stopping to rest and finally he saw the sun. The closer he got to it, the brighter and hotter it was. His hair was singed but still he flew on. At last he was close enough to bite the sun.

The fire dog was a little frightened. He had never seen anything so bright and he had never been so hot. He closed his eyes, opened his mouth wide and bit down on the sun.

"Oh! Oh! It's too hot! Too hot!" yelped the fire dog and he let go of the sun. But the fire dog was proud and he didn't want to disappoint his King. "I'll try again. I'll get it this time," he told himself. He closed his eyes very tight

and bit down hard on the sun. "Oh! It's too hot! It's too hot!" he cried, spitting it out.

Sweating profusely, the fire dog tried over and over to sink his teeth into the burning sun but everytime he had to spit it out. Finally he gave up and returned home.

"Aren't you ashamed, coming home empty-handed?" the King berated the exhausted fire dog. "If you couldn't get the sun, at least you could have gotten the moon."

"Yes, my lord. This time, without fail I'll get you the moon." And with those words the fire dog flew off to steal the moon.

Finally, after several days, the fire dog saw the moon. The closer he got to it, the colder he became. But he flew on for he was determined to take the moon to his King. As soon as he was close enough, the fire dog closed his eyes and bit down hard on the moon.

"Oh! Oh! It's too cold! Too cold!" he cried and let go of the moon. He bit down even harder but he could not hold on because his teeth were too cold. He tried repeatedly until his jaws froze and he was forced to go home without the moon.

The King was furious. "You there!" he called to his second fiercest fire dog. "You go steal the sun. And if you can't get the sun, get the moon."

This dog also returned empty-handed. But the King was determined he would have some light for his dark land. He sent a third fire dog and a fourth and a fifth... He never gave up hope, nor did the kings that came after him.

It is said that eclipses are caused by fire dogs from the Kingdom of Darkness trying to bite the sun and the moon.

The Toad Bridegroom

L
ong ago in a certain village there lived a poor fisherman. One day when he arrived at the lake where he
usually fished he was surprised to see that the water
level was lower than the day before. He fished as usual but
when it came time for him to take his catch to the market
he was disappointed to find that it was considerably less
than usual.

With each passing day the water level dropped lower and
lower and he caught fewer and fewer fish until finally he
arrived one day to find the lake completely empty except
for a very large toad. The fisherman cursed the toad and
then slumped down on the ground, covering his face with
his hands.

The toad hopped up beside the fisherman and said, "Don't
blame me. I didn't eat the fish. But I understand your plight.
You see, I too am in trouble for now I don't have a place
to live. Please let me live with you. Please take me home
with you. I will bring you good fortune."

The fisherman shook his head several times. Then he
picked up his fishing gear and walked home.

That evening the toad came to the fisherman's house and
asked to live there. The fisherman refused at first but finally agreed because his wife begged him to let it stay. She
made a place for it in a corner of the kitchen and fed it
worms and rice.

The toad grew as large as a boy. And as it grew, the

couple learned to love it and often talked to it as they would the child they did not have.

Still, they were not prepared for the request it made one day.

"I would like for you to arrange for me to marry one of your neighbor's daughters," it said. "I think it is about time for me to take a wife."

The fisherman and his wife were flabbergasted. Finally the fisherman said, "Look, we love you as if you were our own son. But you are not a human. And even if you were, there is no way a poor man like I could propose a marriage with such a wealthy family. It's absurd."

"The parents may think it is absurd and object but one of the daughters may think otherwise and accept. You can never tell. Please try. That's all I ask," pleaded the toad.

So the fisherman and his wife went to the wealthy man's house and nervously made their proposal. The man was so angry he struck the fisherman and had his servants throw him and his wife bodily off his premises.

They limped home and sadly told the toad what had happened.

"I'm sorry they treated you badly," said the toad. "But don't worry. I'm sure something good will come of all this. You'll see."

Late that night the toad crept out of the house with a piece of string and a lantern. It tied the lantern to the foot of a hawk which it had caught earlier and made its way stealthily to the rich man's house. It climbed a tall persimmon tree beside the gate, lit the lantern and let the hawk fly to the length of the string. Then it called out in a loud voice, "The master of this house rejected a marriage proposal today. Reconsider or doom will befall this family and all that come after." It repeated this over and over until the man came out into the yard and bowed toward the light.

Then it let go of the string so that the hawk flew away with the lighted lantern.

The man was certain that it was a message from Heaven. He prayed all night for forgiveness. In the morning, he told his oldest daughter to marry the toad but she refused so vehemently that he finally relented. Then he told his second daughter to marry the toad but she too adamantly refused. Finally he told his youngest daughter that she must marry the toad and she agreed without any argument.

The man then called on the fisherman. He apologized for his discourteous behavior and said that he would gladly accept the fisherman's proposal to give one of his daughters to the toad in marriage. The marriage was thus arranged and both families set about preparing for the wedding which would be held in several days.

The wedding was attended by a great crowd of people because word of the marriage spread quickly through the valley. The bride was horrified at the thought of marrying a toad but, knowing that the fate of her family depended on her marriage, she remained composed throughout the ceremony and behaved the way every bride was expected to behave. Even during the feasting that followed the ceremony and continued into the evening, she turned a deaf ear to the rude jokes and comments the guests made and ignored their stares.

Finally, it was time for the newlyweds to retire to the bridal chamber. The bride sat quietly in a corner of the room and tried not to look at her husband as her eyes swelled with tears.

"Please don't be afraid. I won't hurt you," said the toad in a soothing voice. "Don't worry. You have proved yourself to be a loving and righteous girl. Everything will be fine. Now dry your tears and do as I say. Get a knife and cut the skin from my back."

The girl refused at first. But the toad was so persistent that she finally bit her lip and cut a slit down its back. Then, lo and behold, a handsome young prince stepped out.

The next morning the prince put his toad skin on again and he and his bride went outside to greet their parents and the wedding guests. The onlookers were astonished at how radiant the bride looked.

But they were even more astonished when the prince stepped out of his toad skin and revealed his true identity. Then he took his bride and his adopted parents to live in a beautiful palace and they all lived happily ever after.

Why the Sea Is Salty

Hundreds of years ago there was a king who had a very unusual stone hand mill. It looked like any other stone hand mill but it had special powers. All one had to do was say what one wanted and turn it and out would come what had been requested. If gold was requested, gold would come out. If rice was requested, rice would come out. Whatever was requested, the small hand mill would produce it.

A thief made up his mind to steal the hand mill because once he had heard of it he couldn't get it out of his mind. For days and days he thought about how to steal it but he could not come up with a plan.

Then one day he dressed like a scholar and visited a court official who had access to the royal palace. They chatted about this and that and finally the thief said, "I heard that the King buried his strange hand mill in the ground because he doesn't trust his ministers."

"What's that? The King doesn't trust his ministers? Where did you hear such talk?"

"That's what they say in the countryside," said the thief, happy he had sparked the man's interest. "They say the King dug a deep hole and buried the hand mill because he is so afraid that someone will steal it."

"That's nonsense!" said the official. "The King's hand mill is beside the lotus pond in the inner court."

"Oh, is that so?" said the thief, trying to control his excitement.

"No one would dare try to steal the King's hand mill," said the official. "Who would even think of trying when the thing is lying right beside the lotus pond where there is always lots of people coming and going."

The thief was so excited that all he could say was "Yes" and "That's right" until he was able to leave.

For many days the thief studied the situation. Then one very dark night, he climbed the palace wall and stole the hand mill from beside the lotus pond.

He was brimming with pride and confidence as he made his way back to the wall. But once outside the palace, he was overcome with fear of being discovered. His heart skipped a beat every time he met someone on the street. He decided to steal a boat and go to his hometown to hide because he knew that once the theft was discovered, everyone in the city and on the roads would be questioned.

Once at sea the thief lay back against the bow of the boat and laughed. Then he began to sing and dance as he thought about how rich he was going to be. Then he thought about what to request from the hand mill. He did not want to ask for something common and easy to obtain.

"Salt! Salt!" he suddenly shouted. "I'll ask for salt! Everyone needs salt. I can sell it and become a rich man. I'll be the richest man in the country."

He fell down on his knees and began turning the hand mill, singing as he did, "Salt! Salt! Make some salt!" Then he began dancing and singing about being a rich man.

And the hand mill kept turning and turning. Salt spilled over the sides of the small boat but the thief just kept dancing and singing and laughing, all the time thinking about the big house he was going to have and the numerous servants who would serve him lavish meals.

Finally the boat was so full of salt that it sank to the

bottom of the sea. And, since no one has ever told the hand mill to stop, it is still turning and making salt, which is why the sea is salty.

Two Brothers

In times gone by there lived two brothers whose loving ways were the talk of the valley where they lived. They took care of their widowed mother and upon her death they divided everything evenly.

Together they worked diligently from sunup to sundown to produce the most they could from their fields. It never failed that come autumn they had the largest harvest in the valley.

One late autumn evening, after they had spent the afternoon sacking and dividing the last of the rice harvest, the older brother thought, "Brother has lots of expenses since he just got married a few months ago. I think I will put a sack of rice in his storehouse and not tell him. I'm sure he would never accept it if I offered it to him." So, late that night, he put a sack of rice on his A-frame carrier and carried it to his brother's storeroom.

The next day, while tidying up his own storage, the older brother was surprised to find he still had the same number of sacks of rice as he had before taking one to his brother. "That's odd," he said, shaking his head, "I'm sure I took a sack of rice to Brother's house last night." He counted his sacks again. "Well," he said, scratching the back of his head, "I'll just take him another one tonight."

So, late that night, he carried a sack of rice to his brother's house.

The next morning, he was again shocked to find he had

the same number of sacks as before. He shook his head over and over and decided he would take his brother another sack that night.

After a late dinner he loaded the rice on his A-frame and set out for his brother's house. It was a full moon and he could see the path quite clearly. Soon he saw a man carrying something bulky coming down the path.

"Why, Brother!" they both called out at the same time. The two brothers put down their sacks and laughed long and hearty for they both understood the mystery behind their unchanging number of sacks of rice. The younger brother thought his older brother could use the rice because he had a larger family.

The Stubborn Couple

O nce upon a time there was a married couple whose greed and stubbornness made them famous throughout their village. Being equally unyielding and having little common sense, the man and woman were constantly bickering.

One morning a neighbor stopped by their house. "It's my husband's birthday, so I brought you some *ttŏk*.* I hope you will enjoy it."

"Oh, we certainly will. Thank you," the couple called as the woman walked through the gate. However, they were not watching her, they were already eyeing the delicious looking rice cakes.

Without a word, the two began eating the *ttŏk*. They were so greedy, they swallowed the pieces whole, each trying to eat more than the other. Finally, there was only one piece left on the plate and they both looked at it greedily.

Presently the man said, "Let's have a contest to decide who will eat this last piece of *ttŏk*."

"All right. That's a good idea," said the woman. "What shall it be?"

"The first person to say a word loses," said the man.

"And the winner gets to eat the *ttŏk*," said the woman.

---

* *Ttŏk:* small steamed rice cakes often stuffed with beans, chestnuts, sesame or brown sugar and often dusted with toasted soy or embellished with aromatic mugwort.

"No more talking from now."

With their lips closed tight, the two stared at each other and from time to time glanced at the *ttŏk*. The afternoon wore on but still neither spoke. The sun set and the house became dark but the two remained silent.

Presently a thief came into the house. However, the man and woman did not utter a sound, each wanting to win the contest. Of course, the thief was surprised to find someone home in the dark house but since neither uttered a word, he assumed they were blind. Slowly and methodically he went through the couple's belongings and put all their valuables in his bag and left.

Hearing the thief whistle merrily as he went through the gate was too much for the woman. "You're unbelievable!" she shouted at her husband. "How could you sit there and let that thief make off with all our valuables?"

"Well, I guess I'll just eat this now since you said the first word," said the man calmly. And he picked up the last piece of *ttŏk*, popped it in his mouth, chewed it up noisily and swallowed with a big gulp.

The Woodcutter and the Dancing Tiger

Many years ago there was a woodcutter who carried a bamboo flute wherever he went. He would play it when taking a break from chopping wood, when walking to and from home, or whenever he had a free moment. Children would gather around him and sing and dance as he played. Even birds seemed charmed by his music.

One day the woodcutter went very deep into the forest to cut wood. He was surprised by a rustling sound and looked up just in time to see a huge tiger coming toward him. With great speed he scrambled up the nearest tree.

The tiger started up the tree after him but the trunk was too slippery for him to climb. He tried over and over but slid down each time. He sat at the bottom of the tree for a while and then loped off into the forest.

The woodcutter breathed a sigh of relief but his legs were so shaky that he could not climb down. Just when he finally felt calm enough to try, five or six tigers appeared at the bottom of the tree.

The woodcutter watched in horror as they climbed one on top of another in an attempt to reach him. "It looks like I'm doomed to die so I might as well enjoy myself one last time," he told himself, pulling out his flute. *Ppillili, ppillili...* he began to play.

Fortunately for the woodcutter, the tiger at the bottom of the pile had recently eaten a shaman. And, because shamans usually dance when they hear music, he began to dance, making it difficult for the other tigers to keep their balance.

With a loud thump the top tiger fell down on the rocky ground. But the tiger kept dancing. One after another they fell down, until all but the dancing tiger lay unconscious on the ground.

Seeing this the woodcutter played even more fervently until the tiger was dancing around like crazy. Slowly the woodcutter climbed down out of the tree and slipped away into the forest.

A Tiger By the Tail

A scholar traveling by foot to attend a national *kwagŏ* examination stopped to rest by a very large rock. He smoked a pipe of tobacco and enjoyed looking at the mountain scenery.

Deciding to leave, he reached for his walking stick leaning against the rock. It felt strange to his touch so he looked at it and was horrified to find he was holding the tail of a tiger that was sitting on top of the rock against which he was leaning.

He stared at the tiger and the tiger stared at him. Not knowing what to do he held the tiger's tail even tighter. Then he grabbed it with both hands, thinking that he would surely be the tiger's next meal if he let go of its tail.

Of course, this made the tiger mad and he tried to gobble up the scholar. But he couldn't sink his teeth into him. Around and around they ran with the scholar holding the tiger's tail and the tiger snapping at the scholar's rear.

After a while, a monk came down the trail. "*Sŭnim, Sŭnim,*"* called the scholar, "please get my cane that is leaning there and kill this tiger."

"How can I, a monk, take the life of a living thing?" asked the monk.

"Then, *Sŭnim*, you hold his tail and I will kill him," said the scholar.

---

* *Sŭnim:* a title of respect for a Buddhist monk.

"No, it's all the same. I can't help another take the life of a living thing," said the monk, shaking his head.

"*Sŭnim*, I have to shit real bad. So would you please hold this tiger's tail so I can go do it?" asked the scholar.

"Oh, sure. You go ahead. I'll hold it till you come back," said the monk and he took the tail from the scholar.

The scholar picked up his bag and headed down the trail for Hanyang, leaving the monk and the tiger running around and around in a circle.

Returning home after taking the *kwagŏ*, the scholar was surprised to see the monk still holding the tiger's tail. "*Sŭnim*," he called, "I see he's still living!"

"I couldn't kill him now if I wanted to. I don't have the strength," cried the monk.

It is said that to this day the monk and the tiger are still running around in a circle beside a huge rock deep in the mountains.

The Cry of the Cuckoo

A long time ago there was a woman who was very mean to her oldest son's wife. All she did was complain and find fault with her. No matter how good Daughter-in-law did the cooking, the cleaning or the mending, it never pleased her.

Daughter-in-law was so afraid of Mother-in-law that she always kept her head down in her presence and rarely ate in front of her. Yet, Mother-in-law complained that she ate so much and was so wasteful that they were always running out of food. So, because she never got enough to eat, Daughter-in-law was always hungry.

Then one New Year's holiday she had to prepare a lot of *ttŭkkuk.** Every time she served up bowls of the steamy dumpling soup, her mouth watered. But she didn't dare eat any because Mother-in-law had told her not to and she could never tell when she might be watching her.

Finally she could stand it no longer. Her stomach ached from hunger. She served her husband and Mother-in-law some ttŏkkuk and returned to the kitchen. Thinking she was safe, since Mother-in-law was busy eating, she filled a bowl with the hot soup and began to eat. She was eating so hungrily that she didn't hear the door to Mother-in-law's room slide open or the kitchen door open.

---

* *Ttŏkkuk:* a soup (*kuk*) made of rice dumplings (*ttŏk*) that is traditionally eaten on New Year's Day.

Mother-in-law stopped dead in the doorway and gasped. Her face changed several shades of red and her eyes became big and then fiery slits.

Daughter-in-law was so surprised she swallowed the spoonful of piping hot *ttŏk* which she had just put in her mouth. She grabbed her throat and fell over. The poor girl choked to death because the *ttŏk* stuck in her gullet.

The family buried her on a mountain behind their house. When the last shovel of dirt was placed on the burial mound, a bird flew over it and cried, *"Ttŏkkuk ttaemune! Ttŏkkuk ttaemune!"* which literally translates "because of *ttŏkkuk.*" The people at the burial were surprised to hear the bird's cry and decided that Daughter-in-law's spirit had entered the bird.

The bird was a *ppŏkkugi*, a cuckoo, whose cry of *Ppŏkkuk! Ppŏkkuk!* could be interpreted as *Ttŏkkuk! Ttŏkkuk!*

The Face in the Mirror

A long time ago a certain Mr. Kim who lived in a hollow high up in the mountains decided to go to Hanyang, the nation's capital, since he had never been there. His parents and his wife could not discourage him from making the trip and after several days he set out on the long trail.

The trip was very hard but Mr. Kim thought it was well worth the effort. He was enthralled with the sights, sounds and smells of the city and he could not believe the array of remarkable items that could be purchased. The thing that intrigued him most was a palm-size piece of glass in which he could see himself.

After a few days he left for home, taking a few things for his family and a mirror for himself.

At home he told everyone about the interesting things he saw and did in Hanyang but he never mentioned the mirror. That he put away in a box in which he kept various trinkets. From time to time he would take it out and look at himself.

Then one day his wife chanced to come into the room without his knowing. She noticed him looking at something and grinning. "What's that?" she asked.

"Nothing! Nothing!" he said in alarm, all the while his hands were busily trying to put something in his box. "I have to go out to hoe the potatoes."

As soon as she was sure he was gone, she opened the

box. "Now I wonder what this is?" she said, picking up the mirror. She turned it over and over and then held it up to her face for a closer look. "Why that man? How could he? He goes to Hanyang to look around and comes back with this pretty girl."

She was so mad she took the mirror to her mother-in-law and told her everything. "Let me see," said Mother-in-law. She examined the mirror and then held it up to her eyes for a better look. "Oh, my. He didn't bring a pretty woman from Hanyang. He brought a wrinkled old hag. Now why in the world would he do that?" she said, shaking her head back and forth and clicking her tongue.

"No, Mother-in-law. He brought a pretty, young girl. I saw her with my own eyes."

"Well, here, have a look. It's a wrinkled old woman."

"No, it's a pretty young girl," "No, it's an old woman," back and forth the mirror went between the two.

"What's all this racket? What's going on?" asked Father-in-law as he entered the room.

"Well, Father-in-law, I found this small, flat thing Husband brought from Hanyang. You see I was curious when I saw him hiding it. Anyway I looked..."

"She says he has a pretty young woman in it," interrupted Mother-in-law, "but all I can see is an old hag and I can't imagine what he would want with her."

"Give me that thing so I can take a look." Father-in-law rubbed his hands over it and then held it up in front of his face to get a better look. "What's this?" he laughed. "There's no pretty young girl or an old hag. There's only a wrinkled old man." He laughed and then he frowned. "We better put this aside until that fellow comes in. He's got some explaining to do."

Presently the couple's little boy came in and noticed the flat, shiny thing on the floor where his grandfather had placed it. He looked at it and was surprised to see a boy staring at him. He stuck out his tongue and the other boy stuck out his tongue. He frowned and the other did the same. He made an ugly face and an ugly face stared back.

He jumped up and ran outside crying. "Ŭ-ang! Ŭ-ang! He took my marble! Ŭ-ang! Ŭ-ang! He took my marble and..."

"Don't cry! Don't cry!" said a teenager, running over from next door. "That's better. Now tell me who took your marble."

"Him! He did!" said the little boy, through his sniffles, and handed the teenager the mirror.

The teenager looked at the mirror and frowned. "Why you big bully! I'll teach you to bother little kids!" he shouted and hit the "bully" with his fist. *Chaeng!* The mirror shattered and pieces of glass fell to the ground.

The Value of Salt

A long, long time ago the son of a wealthy man fell in love with the daughter of a salt peddler. However, his parents would not hear of his marrying her because at that time society was strictly segregated into classes according to occupation and peddling salt was among the lowest.

To his parents' great embarrassment, the young man stubbornly refused any marriage they tried to arrange, saying he would not marry if he could not marry the daughter of the salt peddler. He was so adamant that his parents finally consented and the two married.

However, the girl was constantly abused by her in-laws. Despite her husband's constant protests, they called her names and made snide remarks about her appearance. But, even though she wept inwardly, she never complained, not even to her husband, and diligently went about her daily chores.

Her parents were very sad to learn how she was treated. One day her mother said to her father, "I wish there was something we could do to make life better for her. I can't eat or sleep for thinking about how unhappy she must be living in that house where everyone looks down on her. There must be something we could do...."

"I have an idea," she said after a while. "Let's invite her parents-in-law to dinner."

"Do you really think they would come?" chortled the salt

peddler.

"If we insist, I think they will. But we must insist. And this is what I plan to do..." she explained.

"Well, let's give it a try," agreed the salt peddler.

The in-laws laughed when they received the dinner invitation and flatly refused. But the salt peddler and his wife were so insistent that they finally agreed.

The salt peddler and his wife humbly welcomed the in-laws into their home. As was the custom, the salt peddler and the father-in-law sat down to drink. The salt peddler poured the father-in-law a cup of wine and the father-in-law filled the salt peddler's cup and they drank. Of course, after a drink, the father-in-law ate one of the delicacies the salt peddler's wife had prepared for *anju*.* He could not believe how strange it tasted. It was so bland he could not eat another bite.

Meanwhile, the wife placed a table of food in front of the mother-in-law. The mother-in-law ate some rice and then ate a morsel from one of the side dishes. It was bland. She ate a spoonful of soup. It was also tasteless. She ate a piece of *kimch'i*.** It too was tasteless. It seemed that none of the food was seasoned. She put down her spoon and chopsticks, indicating she was finished eating.

"Please eat some more," said the salt peddler's wife. "You've hardly eaten a bite."

"Oh, I can't. I'm still full from breakfast," said the mother-in-law.

"Here, have another drink," said the salt peddler, extending his empty cup to the father-in-law.

---

* *Anju:* dishes that are always served with liquor.

* * *Kimch'i:* a pungent, fermented dish generally comprising cabbage and turnip seasoned with salt, garlic, leeks, ginger, red chilli pepper and shellfish.

"Oh, no, no," said the father-in-law. "I can't eat another bite so there's no way I can drink."

"Well, I have something to say," said the salt peddler, and he took a deep breath. "I know that you are not eating because the food is tasteless. It is tasteless because it doesn't have a single grain of salt in it. My wife deliberately made it that way to show you how indispensable salt is to our diet. As you have just experienced, it is difficult to eat without it. The King must have salt. Wealthy people like you must have salt. Even a beggar must have salt. Everyone must have salt to make food palatable. And there must be someone to make it available for them. Just as there must be farmers, there must be merchants and there must be rulers. If everyone had a choice, do you think there would be any farmers? Or salt peddlers? Or butchers? What kind of world would it be without them? And what kind of world would it be without salt? I know that I am speaking out of place, but I wanted to explain to you the value of salt and ask you to love my daughter."

The parents-in-law stood up and bowed low to the salt peddler and his wife. "You're absolutely right. No matter how wealthy a person is, he can't live without salt," said the father-in-law in a humble voice. "And thank you for showing me that we all need each other to get along in this world."

And from that time on the wealthy family and the salt peddler's family visited back and forth often and the wealthy couple loved their daughter-in-law and had only words of praise for her.

The Vengeful Snake

T here once dwelt in the city of Hanyang an archer who was famous for his great strength and valor. He lived near Ogansumun, an opening in the city wall through which the Ch'ŏnggyech'ŏn canal flowed.

One afternoon when the archer was taking a walk, he noticed a very large snake coming through the Ogansumun. On second look, he saw that it was stuck with its head through the iron bars of the gate.

The archer quickly set an arrow in his bow and sent it into the snake's head. He then pulled the snake through the bars and beat it to a pulp.

Shortly thereafter the archer's wife conceived and bore a son. Strangely, the baby cried whenever the archer came near or looked at it. As it grew it had nothing to do with him. This upset the archer and he grew to hate his son and became very suspicious of him.

One day the archer and the boy were alone in the house. The archer lay down on the floor to rest. He covered his face with his sleeve but in such a way that he could keep an eye on the boy.

The boy glared at his father for a few minutes. Then, thinking him asleep, he got a knife and stabbed at him. However, the archer rolled over and the knife stuck in the floor. He jumped to his feet and struck the boy on the head with such force it knocked him against the wall and he fell to the floor unconscious. The archer then beat him to death with a stick and left the house.

Presently the archer's wife returned and found her child dead. She fell to her knees and wept. After a while she covered the broken body with a quilt to await the archer's return. Soon, to her dismay, the quilt began to move. Thinking the boy had revived, she happily pulled back the quilt. She screamed and rushed out of the house. A huge snake lay where her son's body had been.

The archer returned at sundown and was met at the gate by his distraught wife. She told him about the snake.

Carefully he entered the house and looked into the room where he had slain his son. A huge snake lay coiled, ready to strike, on the floor in the center of the room. On its head was a scar made by an arrow.

The archer spoke slowly and solemnly. "I am sorry. We were not enemies, so it was wrong for me to shoot you. But to transform yourself into my son to get revenge is even worse. It proves that my suspicions of you were correct." After a slight pause, the archer said, "You became my son in order to kill me, your father. Should I, in turn, kill you, my son?"

The snake seemed to bow its head a bit. "You've had your revenge and you've returned to your original form. Let's forget the past," said the archer and he opened the door. "Now leave, please."

The snake slithered out the door. It went straight to the Ogansumun and slid through the bars.

When the Buddha Wept Blood

here was once a village which flourished by the sea.
It even had a port where not only fishing boats but
also trading ships docked. Unfortunately, its residents
became lazy and enjoyed nothing more than drinking wine
and joking.

There was a kindly old woman who ran a small tavern
near the waterfront. It was always packed with customers
so she made a good living.

One day, just after she opened the tavern doors to prepare for the first onslaught of customers, an old man in
tattered clothes came into the tavern. "Excuse me, I can see
you're just opening, but do you have something I could eat?
I'm very hungry," he said very humbly.

The old woman could tell from his appearance that he
could not pay, but she told him to sit down and she would
get him something. She served him a large bowl of rice,
a bowl of soup, a roasted fish, several side dishes and a
bowl of rice wine.

The man ate hungrily. And when he finished, he wiped
his mouth with his hand, stood up and slowly said, "That
was very good. Thank you very much. But...I'm very sorry. I don't have any money. How can I pay you?"

"Think nothing of it," said the old woman. "You were
hungry and I fed you. I was glad to be able to do it."

The man didn't move. He stared at the old woman's face

as though in a daze. Then he blurted out, "Let me tell you something important. Start preparing enough food to do you for four days. And, when that stone Buddha on the mountain in front of here weeps blood, take the food to the top of that mountain and stay there. If you don't you will surely die. I read it in your face." So saying, the man left.

The old woman did not question what the fortuneteller told her but immediately began preparing food supplies. And, several times throughout the day, she climbed up the mountain to see if the Buddha was crying or not.

Thinking she should not keep this information to herself, she told the fortuneteller's words to all the men who came into the tavern so that they could survive whatever catastrophe was to befall them.

The men only laughed and made jokes about "the crazy old woman." Then a man said, "Let's play a trick on her. What do you say we..." The other men agreed and so that evening they went up the mountain and painted red tears on the stone Buddha.

The next morning, shortly after sunrise, the men went to the tavern. They banged on the door and shouted, "It's happened! It's happened! The Buddha is crying tears of blood!"

The old woman opened the door and shouted at the men, "You should get going! Quick! Head up the mountain!"

"We will," said one of the men. "But first we have to prepare some food. You go on first."

The old woman put the bundle of food she had prepared on her head and hurried off.

The men watched her go up the mountain until she was out of sight and then they went into the tavern.

"Let's drink up," shouted one of the men. "The place is ours."

Even though it was early morning, the men began to drink

and laugh about the trick they had played on the old woman. They had emptied many jugs of wine when they suddenly heard a roaring sound. They threw open the tavern doors just in time to see a huge wave rolling toward them. In a flash they realized that the old woman was right. But it was too late.

The sea crashed down on the men, the tavern and everything around it. The whole village was swept away by the tidal wave and swallowed up by the sea. The old woman was the only survivor.

While the Axe Handle Rots

Once upon a time a woodcutter went deep into the mountains to cut wood. He worked so hard that he did not notice a storm blowing up until big raindrops began to pelt him. Quickly he took cover under a large crag.

To amuse himself, he began to study the rock face and soon discovered a hole just large enough for a man to pass through. In the blink of an eye, he climbed through, thinking he would be better protected from the wind and pelting rain.

When his eyes adjusted to the darkness, he was surprised to find that he was in a large cave, the end of which he couldn't see. Being a curious sort, he decided to explore.

He went deeper and deeper into the cave. Then he became aware of a dull slapping sound. A few steps later he saw a faint glow in the distance. The slaps became crisper the closer he got to the light.

And when he came to the source of the light, he received quite a shock. For there, sitting on the floor, playing *paduk** were two old men with long white beards dressed in an outmoded fashion. He knew at once that they were

---

* *Paduk:* commonly known by its Japanese name *Go*, it is a board game for two played with black and white stone counters.

*shinsŏn.***

As they played, neither man uttered a word. The stillness was broken only by the sound of the *paduk* pieces being slapped down on the game board.

Little by little the woodcutter's awe and fear subsided. Step by step he moved closer to the men until he was beside them. Quietly he watched them play. Then he felt a hunger pain.

As if reading his thoughts, one of the men handed him a bowl of wine and the other handed him a piece of food from a small table beside them. And in unison they said, "Eat and enjoy."

The woodcutter ate the food and drank the wine as he watched them play. Both were very delicious and gave him a pleasant feeling.

"I better hurry home," he muttered after a while. "I wonder if the rain has stopped?"

Thinking thus he reached for his axe which he had leaned against the wall. But the handle crumbled in his hand. "That's strange," he muttered as he left the hall. "Those two must have played a trick on me."

He was glad to finally climb out of the hole into the bright sunlight. He looked around but there was not a trace of rain. "The rain certainly dried fast," he told himself as he rushed home.

When he arrived, he had another shock. For he found his family holding a memorial to mark the second anniversary of his death.

Once they were over the shock of seeing him alive, they explained that he had disappeared two years ago; that he had not returned from cutting wood and, when their search

---

Shinsŏn: Taoist immortals said to live a carefree life in secluded mountains or on remote islands.

proved futile, they presumed he had been eaten by a wild animal. On hearing his story, they decided that he had fallen under the spell of Taoist hermits. Thus comes the saying, "While enjoying the life of *shinsŏn*, the axe handle rots."

Bibliography

Although this list includes books that have no relation to Korean stories, they were a source of inspiration.

Carpenter, Frances. *Tales of a Korean Grandmother.* Garden City: Doubleday and Company, Inc., 1947.

Comber, Leon. *Oriental Stories.* Singapore: Graham Brash, 1989.

_____. *More Oriental Stories.* Singapore: Graham Brash, 1989.

Gale, James S. *Korean Folk Tales: Imps, Ghosts and Fairies.* Tokyo: Charles E. Tuttle Company, 1971.

Kim Ho-gun and Yun Yol-su. *Han-guk horang-i (The Korean Tiger).* Seoul: Yolhwadang, 1986.

Kim Sa-rim. *Han-guk chŏllae tonghwa (Korean Fairy Tales),* Vols.1-10. Uam Publishing Company, 1988.

Korean Cultural Studies Society, Kathleen J. Crane Foundation. *The Morning Bright.* Seoul: Ewha Womans University Press, 1990.

Minford, John. *Favourite Folktales of China.* Singapore: Graham Brash, 1988.

O'Brien, Joanne. *Chinese Myths and Legends.* London: Arrow Books, 1990.

Riordan, James. *An Illustrated Treasury of Fairy and Folk Tales.* Twickenham: The Hamlyn Publishing Group Ltd., 1986.

Seki, Keigo. *Folktales of Japan.* Chicago: The University of Chicago Press, 1963.

Seros, Kathleen. *Sun and Moon: Fairy Tales From Korea.* Seoul: Hollym International Corporation, 1982.

Zŏng In-Sŏb. *Folk Tales from Korea.* Seoul: Hollym International Corporation, 1979.